# Final Departure

# FINAL DEPARTURE

**Jeff Walton**

**Final Departure** by Jeff Walton
© 2018 Jeff Walton. All rights reserved.

ISBN: 978-0-9974334-2-5 (Hardcover)
ISBN: 978-0-9974334-0-1 (Paperback)
ISBN: 978-0-9974334-1-8 (Kindle)

Sunbrook Publishing
PO Box 730
St. Augustine, FL 32085
www.JeffWaltonBooks.com
JeffWaltonBooks@gmail.com

Disclaimer: This book is a work of fiction. Names, characters, businesses, organizations, places, incidents and events are the product of the author's imagination, or are used fictitiously. Any resemblance to actual persons, living or dead, or actual events is entirely coincidental.

Book Cover Design: Rik Feeney / www.RickFeeney.com
Stock Photography: © Khunaspix | Dreamstime.com

# Dedication

*To my Creator, King, and Counselor.*

Final Departure

# Contents

# PREFACE

This book is a warning. Although the characters and plot are fictional, the core subject matter is not. It's meant to be a wake-up call for many of us who have fallen asleep spiritually and are marching toward an eternity without an exit plan.

This is not a book about how to play church. It's designed to focus you, the reader, on what many believe to be reality. At the heart of the existence of every one of us is our need to receive unconditional love. I believe we have only one true source of love that can satisfy us—our Creator.

My generation, the baby boomers, have become the worst-case-scenario crowd. Unless we believe a threat is real, we don't take it seriously. The intent of this book is to make you reconsider what you believe to be the true nature of our universe and the essence of our existence.

Our choice, while we exist on this earth, is to decide whether we will seek, find, and nurture God's love for us. While we can freely reject God's love, I believe the choice will result in consequences beyond our comprehension.

We can choose to open our eyes, our minds, and our hearts, and consider the evidence all around us. Maybe, just maybe, our life on this earth is not all there is after all. The choice is yours. I hope you take the choice seriously.

Final Departure

# CHAPTER ONE

## *The Perfect Storm*

Dan Lucas nimbly weaved his way through a thick crowd of passengers streaming along Charlotte Douglas International Airport's busy concourse. Although running late, he'd made up his mind not to miss his flight. He pondered the possibility that his flight might get out before the storm gathered full strength.

What should have been a fairly routine return trip home was becoming a major quest. He forced himself not to worry about what might happen. He pushed forward through the throng of preoccupied travelers. While he surveyed the crowd, he realized he hadn't called his wife to let her know he'd made it back to the States, safe and sound.

Dan yearned to be home. He was on the final leg of his trip from Germany. He'd endured the ten-hour flight from Frankfurt with stoic endurance, but jet lag was threatening to shut him down. He'd spent over an hour going through immigration and customs, all the while thinking about home.

A dull headache began to throb in his temples, and his eyes let him know they needed sleep—something he couldn't do on the cramped flight he'd just left.

Sensing he needed a place to collapse with his bag, he scanned the gate area looking for a seat that met his requirements. It had to be a seat against the wall so he could see everyone who approached—a habit acquired from many years of looking for people who might mean harm. He spotted an empty end seat in a row next to the terminal's wall, near an exit door; he moved quickly to take the only acceptable option.

An announcement interrupted his thoughts: "Ladies and gentlemen, Flight 1891, with nonstop service to Jacksonville, Florida, is delayed until further notice because of weather. We'll update you as soon as we have new information, but until ground operations can clear the runways, all departing flights are grounded."

Dan reached for his cell phone to call his wife and tell her the bad news. Gone a month and now more delays. *After more than thirty-five years of moving and traveling for my career, this is how I spend my retirement?*

Dan felt a pang of regret and a blistering lack of self-confidence in his decision making. *I'm supposed to be doing something helpful to others—not chasing the almighty buck.*

\*\*\*

The truck radio crackled... "And now, for an extreme weather update. A late winter arctic air mass is pushing down from Canada and has much of the Midwest in its icy grip. This system is already being blamed for more than a dozen deaths in Missouri, and as the frigid air pushes southeast and collides with some unusually warm gulf air, we could see some very dangerous icy conditions, especially in Tennessee, Kentucky, and parts of the Carolinas. This storm has the potential to be a historic ice event. We'll have an update for you at the top of the hour."

The word *ice* caught the nervous driver's attention. Ice meant trouble, especially for a tanker truck loaded with gasoline. He had to know what he was facing in the miles ahead. As a gust of wind buffeted the cab, Rob tightened his grip on the wheel. Then a few telltale droplets of icy rain pelted the windshield.

*Damn, it's here.*

He glanced down at his speedometer. He had to make his last delivery before the roads were impassable.

\*\*\*

"Keep your mouth shut! You're not goin' anywhere!"

The woman sobbed softly as she leaned her head against the pickup's cold passenger-door window. The tightly cinched cable tie on her wrists cut the circulation.

"Will you stop? I need some time to think!" The young man's words were slightly slurred, and as he reached for a pack of cigarettes on the dash, his hand shook.

"I can't believe this—I can't hardly see where I'm going. Can anything else go wrong with my life?" he screamed at the windshield.

The young woman sniffed and cleared her throat. "This isn't going to help anything. Your dad's plane is probably gone already. You need to stop this, don't you understand?"

He whipped up the ramp and onto the interstate, cutting off a Greyhound bus as he yanked the banged-up red pickup truck into the middle lane of traffic. His passenger whimpered in fear.

He mumbled, "Maybe the storm slowed things down."

Going much too fast, the pickup started to drift into a skid to the right. Not fazed, the driver used his skills acquired in the harsh winters of the Northeast and eased off the gas pedal and turned smoothly into the skid to straighten it out. Within a few seconds, the truck's path became straight.

"I need to talk to him before he leaves. He'll listen this time. You'll see, he'll help me out and we'll get back to like we used to be."

The young woman began to sob again. "The way you're driving; we'll be killed trying to get there. You, me, and the baby."

\*\*\*

Dan's wife answered on the third ring.

"Hi, hon," he said. "I'm here in Charlotte. Made it back okay, but my connecting flight's been delayed because of weather. Looks like we're getting an ice storm. I don't think we'll get out of here tonight, but they haven't told us the flight's been cancelled—at least not yet. The storm is starting to get really bad."

"I'm sorry, Dan. I was looking forward to seeing you tonight. It's been so long. You keep me posted, okay? Did you eat?"

"Not yet, but I will as soon as I find out what's happening with the flight."

Connie's long sigh came through the phone. "Love you," she said.

He could hear the smile in her voice. Lord, how he missed her. "I love you too, honey." He ended the call.

14

He was rapidly reaching the stage where he was so tired, he'd get a headache instead of sleep; but until he knew one way or the other about the flight, he'd have to stay near the gate.

As he was putting away his phone, Dan caught a glimpse of a gentleman in the distance, laboring toward his row of seats. He wore baggy khaki pants that were draped over oxblood penny loafers, giving him a frumpy, dated look.

Dan didn't know what about the man captured his attention. In Dan's line of work, there was usually a reason, but this older man didn't send off danger signals. *Some sort of academic or middle-management professional, I'll bet. He almost laughed out loud.*

The man put down his briefcase and dropped with a heavy thud into the seat next to Dan. Dan could smell fresh smoke on his clothing and noticed yellowish nicotine stains on his thick, short fingers.

"Had to go all of the way out of the terminal. No smoking room anywhere inside. It's getting nasty out. I think this flight's in trouble," he said, mostly out of breath. He spoke with a deep nasal voice, but the speech had an air of authority and restrained aggression.

*He could be as tired as I am. Who knows?* Dan nodded and said, "Yeah, just heard the weather. Looks like a major ice storm is moving in from the northwest. Ice storms are worse than snow."

"You've got that right," the man said. His resignation and annoyance were evident.

Before Dan could reply, the loudspeaker came on as a disembodied airline employee delivered the news nobody wanted to hear. "Ladies and gentlemen, we have been

15

informed that Flight 1891 to Jacksonville has been cancelled. A new flight has been scheduled with a departure time of 7:00 a.m. tomorrow. We have been advised that some roads in the area have been temporarily closed because of icing. We will update you on road conditions when we have new information. Anyone in need of lodging can check with the information desk in the atrium or in the baggage claim area to determine which hotels are still accessible."

"Looks like we'll be sleeping in the terminal," Dan said aloud, and shook his head as the reality settled in. After sleeping poorly for a month on thin German mattresses, he now resigned himself to the idea of sitting in a seat all night. "Won't help this jet lag much."

"I can't sleep on these seats," the gentleman beside him moaned while he fished around in his open briefcase. "My back will never take it."

"I don't think we have many good options," Dan quipped. He'd gotten adept at accepting circumstances he couldn't control or change, but he understood his fellow traveler's distress.

"I think I'll stretch my legs," Dan announced as he tossed his jacket on the seat. "Could you save my seat, please?"

The man nodded while staring at the pages of a dog-eared paperback.

"Thanks," Dan muttered, and slung his backpack over his shoulder. He thought about moving to another seat that would have more room and privacy, but something about the man intrigued him.

*Hope I don't regret it.*

# CHAPTER TWO

## *What's My Line?*

The rhythmic scraping of the wipers on the tanker truck's windshield kept the driver alert as he strained to see through the mostly ice-crusted glass. Darkness had come quickly with the storm.

He needed to make this last delivery and get home. He needed the money for sure. And despite the worsening ice storm, the trucker barreled ahead on Interstate 85, now just a few miles north of the Charlotte Douglas International Airport. He'd had delays. Cars had piled up on the ice for the last fifteen miles.

He only slightly slowed as he began to negotiate the exit ramp to Little Rock Road. The truck's tires barely kept a grip on the increasingly slick road as he headed south, on to hotel row and toward his final destination, the Airport Express Gas Station.

Ahead, he saw the taillights of several cars that had tangled in an accident, blocking his lane. He downshifted and decelerated his rig to make a turn onto a service road next to a hotel, hoping to find an alternate route. As he glanced at his strangely silent GPS to make sure it was still working, his female digital companion's voice announced, "Recalculating." He maneuvered his rig through a parking lot and noticed an exit ahead.

"Turn left onto Keeter Drive."

He dutifully followed the GPS directions and turned onto the two-land road, confident that he had found an alternate route around the multi-car pileup. Momentarily relieved, he pressed down on the accelerator.

Out of nowhere, a red pickup shot alongside and cut in front of him, fishtailing on the slick roadway.

"Oh my God!" he shouted to the crucifix swinging from his mirror.

He was going much too fast to brake on the icy asphalt. Out of the corner of his eye, he saw a driveway on his right. Purely out of reflex, he aimed his truck at the mass of industrial buildings, lightly tapping the brakes, praying he'd find an open space to bring his rig to a safe stop.

He frantically downshifted his rig as he steered around the complex to the right, looking for an exit road. His headlights caught the back of the facility's lot, letting him know he was trapped. When he thought all was lost, he noticed a clearing in the trees on his left. He jerked the wheel hard—too hard. The rig miraculously made the left turn but began to rock back and forth. Rob had no idea where the clearing would lead, but he continued to tap the brakes, slowly reducing his speed. Up ahead, he caught the first glimpse of what awaited him.

"No, no, no, no—"

He mashed the brake pedal, sending the multi-ton tanker—about half full of gasoline—into an out-of-control skid over the frozen ground. The slick coat of freezing rain provided the perfect friction reducer.

The truck glided through the clearing like a mammoth toboggan, barely missing large trees on either side of the open area. With nothing of substance to decrease the sliding truck's momentum, it plowed through some small saplings and bushes and ripped through a chain-link fence, where it slammed head-on into an electrical substation.

The violent crash spun the truck a full 180 degrees, causing it to continue skidding until the back of the truck crashed into a second transformer. Live transmission lines fell on the rig, sending a shower of sparks high into the air.

In a split second, the collision ripped open the trailer's multi-layer tank, sending thousands of gallons of gasoline gushing onto the icy ground and into the surrounding transformer farm. A huge fireball erupted into the air.

The resulting flames and surge of thousands of volts seared the tail end of the truck and ignited secondary fires in pools of gas that had collected on the ground. Within seconds, the substation was a massive conflagration, and acrid flames and white-blue sparks shot high into the icy night.

\*\*\*

Dan strode through the busy terminal searching for food. The lights flickered for a few seconds and returned to full brightness. He spotted a take-out kiosk selling southern barbecue—something he'd been craving for a month.

After nearly inhaling a plate of beef brisket, Dan finished an iced tea and then carefully cleaned the tabletop with a napkin. Full and even drowsier, he felt a sense of deep fatigue—not just from a lack of sleep—but from a weariness of working far too long in a rigorous and dangerous profession. Gone was the spark of adventure and the belief that tomorrow would bring a more fulfilling day. Dan knew it was time to retire—completely—and start a new phase in his life.

He smiled. After years of study, he was finally ready to get his book written. It was more than something he wanted to do now; it seemed almost a calling. He looked forward to holding his grandchildren, laughing with his daughters and wife, and doing what God wanted him to do at this stage of his life. He wasn't over the hill yet, even if he did feel a hundred years old some days.

He shook himself out of his thoughts and gazed across the atrium where a young family caught his eye. He recognized the look. The neatly trimmed short haircut and crisp dress of the man were a sure giveaway. *Another military family being transferred.*

Making eye contact, Dan motioned for the young man and his wife and children to come take his table. As the family walked toward Dan, a heavyset man and two younger women pushed their way to the table and reached to grab the stools.

Dan swung his body around to block the man's access while he cradled the tabletop with his arms.

"This table's taken," he said clearly.

"What do you mean?" whined the man.

Dan turned his head and shot him a menacing glance while he tightened his grip on the table. "Like I said, this table's taken."

The man whiffed a grunt of complaint and retreated with the two women, who were red-faced. Dan stood steady and turned toward the advancing couple with their two small children.

"You folks look like you could use a place to sit. Military?" he asked with a smile.

"Yes, sir. I guess we're pretty obvious." The man spoke with a noticeable southern drawl. He glanced nervously at the departing trio as he held his young son, and then looked back at Dan. "Thanks for the table."

"No problem. I'm finished anyway," Dan answered as if nothing had happened. "I've been through what you're going through, many times. Where you headed?"

"Naples, Italy, sir. I'm being assigned to the Naval Support Site."

"Ah, Italy, a beautiful country. You'll like it there."

Dan wished the family well and offered words of encouragement about their transfer and adventures to come. Dan felt sorry for them, knowing what a trying night they'd have with their small children. He volunteered to watch their kids while they went to get some food, but the couple politely declined and thanked him for his kindness. With a wave, he hefted his pack over his shoulder and headed back, in no hurry, toward the departure gate.

Somehow he and Connie had made it through all of their transfers unscathed, but now he sensed he no longer had the patience or endurance to undergo uprooting the family every few years and moving to a strange new home, often in a foreign country. She'd accepted every change of duty station with grace and devotion, managing their young children and worldly possessions almost single-handedly when he was already in place.

He'd made his decision. Gone was the spark to seek out new adventures. He felt settled now and had no desire to search for something better. *No more moving up the career ladder, building new empires, and saving the world one more time.*

He arrived at his seat. Picking up his jacket, he nodded his thanks to the man, who barely acknowledged him. As Dan slid his backpack to the floor and slipped into his seat, the loudspeaker again clamored for their attention.

"Ladies and gentlemen, we have an update. Because of icing and unsafe road conditions, the airport has been closed to all inbound and outbound vehicular traffic. All passengers are requested to stay in the terminal for safety reasons, until further notice. We are sorry for the inconvenience."

"Looks like it's going to be a long night," Dan commented in an effort to break the ice.

After a long silence, he started to regret his decision to return to the same seat.

"Where're you coming from?" Dan directed the question in the gentleman's direction as he dug through his pack for his notebook. *Might as well get some work done until I can sleep.*

"Philadelphia." The man's answer was curt, and long in coming.

"What takes you to Jacksonville?" Dan forced out the question, hoping to start a conversation, though he wasn't sure why.

The man closed his book and squinted at Dan with an expression of supreme annoyance. "I'm going to see my daughter in Palm Coast."

"You must make this trip often," Dan commented, ignoring the man's obvious agitation. *Why do I feel a need to pursue this?*

The man slowly shook his head. Resigned to his forced interrogation, he answered. "This is my first trip to Florida. I haven't seen her in years." The raspy reply didn't hide the man's irritation.

Dan could hear pellets of icy rain popping as they pelted the terminal windows, which were quickly becoming opaque with a growing coat of ice. He decided not to push his annoyed neighbor any further. He opened his notebook and squinted at his neat printing. His eyes were too tired to focus, though. He put the notebook in his pack and pulled out a soda he had bought on the way to his seat. Maybe it would help his rapidly dropping blood sugar levels.

"I brought some sodas back from the food court. I have a diet and a regular. Like one?" he asked his reluctant "roommate."

The man glanced up with a surprised look and answered, "Why, yes, a regular."

After taking a swig and wiping his mouth with the back of his hand, he turned toward Dan. "What takes *you* to Jacksonville?" the man asked in a quiet, flat tone.

By now, the row of seats next to them was empty. Dan felt more comfortable talking without others within earshot.

"I live there. I'm getting back from some work overseas."

"What do you do for a living?"

"Security-related contract work. Most of my work is with the Department of Defense. I retired a couple of years ago from federal law enforcement."

"You don't look old enough to be retired," the older man retorted. "But then, the government works differently than the rest of us. Who did you work for?"

"Naval Criminal Investigative Service. NCIS. It's a civilian agency in the Department of the Navy."

"I see. So you're a criminal investigator?"

"Yeah. I spent most of my career doing counterintelligence and combating terrorism." Dan lifted the hand with the soda in it. "Mandatory retirement at fifty-seven. They force us into the world to find other work."

"Can't say I've ever met someone in federal law enforcement before. What made you decide on that career field?"

"I first heard about NCIS when I was in the navy on active duty. In those days it was NIS, the Naval Investigative Service."

"But you said it was a civilian agency, right?"

"Yes, it is. NCIS agents are civilians hired directly by the Department of the Navy. In my case, I was drafted during the Vietnam War and my first contact with NCIS was while I was a sailor on active duty. They approached me to work undercover drug ops for them. Drugs were a major problem for the armed services in that war."

The man shivered and took another swig of soda. "Sounds dangerous."

"In hindsight it was, but at the time it was exciting."

"Yes," the man said, "drugs were everywhere in those days, especially on campuses. A lot of the army was stoned, too. It wasn't just the sailors." A slight smile lightened his expression.

"That's right, and drugs were cheap in Asia in those days too. I spent a lot of time in bars and back alleys in places like Hong Kong, Thailand, and Indonesia, making drug buys and setting up the traffickers for arrests with the host country's law enforcement. Word of the drug busts traveled fast in Asian ports. After a few dealers were arrested, everyone stopped selling to Americans."

"You seem to have emerged unscathed from the experience."

"I'm not sure about that. But I loved the excitement and the adventure, and I realized I'd found my future career. After the year of undercover work with NCIS, I got out of the navy, went to college, and was hired by NCIS in the early '80s."

"You said you did counterintelligence work. How did you get from buying drugs to counterintelligence?"

Dan finished his soda and tucked the can on the floor by his feet. "When I started with NCIS as a new special agent, I did mostly criminal cases for the first year, but an opportunity came up to do some CI work, as we call it, and I jumped at the chance. Ended up doing it for most of my career. Not long after, I started doing combating terrorism work, too."

"Now that you're retired, do you think you made the right choice?" the man asked.

"I do. CI and CT can save lives and protect a country." Dan shifted in his seat and extended his hand to the man from Philadelphia. "Name's Dan Lucas. Nice to meet you."

The man reached over the empty seats and shook Dan's hand. "My name's Ben Chernick."

"So, what do you do, Ben?"

"I'm a sociology professor."

*I knew it!* Dan thought, and fought back a smile. He asked, "What got you into teaching?"

"It was the logical step to take at the time. When I was doing some student teaching, I got some positive comments from the undergrads, so I guess you could say I found my calling, too. Teaching came to me naturally and I enjoyed it. A professor on the faculty saw that I was doing well and offered to help get me a teaching job. Like you, the rest is history. Now I'm tenured and planning to stay put as long as I'm alive and functional."

"You must like teaching."

"Used to—and still do at the graduate level. But the undergrad classes are not as much fun as they used to be. Maybe it's because I'm getting older and can't relate to the students like before. I can't see me doing anything else, though; the die is cast."

"Well, I appreciate hearing about your career."

Ben nodded and then looked closely at Dan. "You know, I'm curious about something, Dan. You were in Vietnam. You were still in the service after the war, right? What was your take on the war?"

Dan thought a moment. He'd bet his ticket home that he and Ben had very different world views. But the man had asked ....

"It was really a proxy war. The retreat of America from Vietnam was clearly in the best interest of what was then the Soviet Union. I'm sure you're aware that in those days, Russia and China were major allies, and North Vietnam's Ho Chi

26

Minh started his operations in China. From all that I've read, in addition to their huge material support to the Viet Cong, the Soviets, through assets in the international media, helped shape public opinion with false articles planted in the news, to turn the world against America's role in the war. From where I sat then, I saw it had worked. Public support for our involvement eroded, our politicians lost their will, and we pulled out."

"I don't think the press had much of an impact," said Ben. "People knew the war was bad. Why fight a war on the other side of the world when you haven't been attacked at home?

"You have to draw the line somewhere, and I think that line should be when a large number of people are faced with genocide. Many hundreds of thousands of South Vietnamese were killed by the North after we left. That treaty was a farce and so was our withdrawal."

Ben looked thoughtful. "There are two sides to every story, aren't there? The truth and then everything else."

The lights flickered again and Dan watched the color drain out of Ben's face.

"Yes, sir, that's a pretty accurate statement," Dan replied softly.

# CHAPTER THREE

## *Leap of Faith*

"Richie, listen to me. You need to cut me loose. I can't feel my hands. Let's talk about this. You can't keep driving around like a crazy man. You'll kill us or someone else. That poor truck driver almost ran us over. Stop this now," she begged.

"If you don't shut up, I'm going to gag you," he said in a rough, deep tone. He slowed the vehicle a couple miles per hour and glanced at the fuel gauge." I'll find us something to eat. And I'll loosen your hands. I don't need you running away, get that? I need gas. Damned storm. I need to find another way to the airport."

He slammed his open palm against the steering wheel and his passenger jumped. He was shaking like a sapling in a hurricane. He squinched his eyes to be able to see her through his tears. When she opened her mouth to speak, he whispered, "Oh, shut up."

\*\*\*

Pulses of brilliance from the emergency vehicles' strobe lights bounced off millions of droplets of frozen rain and illuminated the dark sky like miniature camera flashes. As firefighters from Haz Mat One and other units fought to douse the flames engulfing much of the substation, a crew from Rescue 10 used the Jaws of Life to pry open the mangled truck cab.

After more than an hour, the rescue team freed the badly mutilated remains of the driver. Although the body was burned beyond recognition, the driver's back pants pocket was still partially intact. A responding officer used large tweezers to pull out the remnant of a charred leather wallet and placed it in a ventilated evidence bag.

Despite the nearly impassable roads near the crash site, Duke Energy technicians had braved the frigid night air to help direct the firefighters in an effort to control the damage to the transformers, some of which were still leaking oil. The battle to smother the flames with foam as quickly as possible had to be won to prevent any more transformer damage. The storm had already caused numerous trees to fall and take out power lines, and now broad swaths of the Charlotte area were blanketed by rolling darkness with the loss of the substation. The Charlotte airport was potentially next.

Several TV reporters cloistered outside of the crash scene's perimeter dabbed on makeup under the cover of handheld umbrellas. They soon stared into the glare of camera lights and prepared to tape action cam reports of the massive crash for the 11:00 o'clock news.

*** 

Dan had just gotten comfortable when the lights flickered in the terminal and went off. Ben let out a groan.

"Are you all right?" Dan asked.

Ben didn't answer as he pulled out a lighter and frantically flicked it.

"Wouldn't do that if I were you; you'll get tossed out of here."

"I need the light," Ben gasped. "The dark's bad for my heart."

Just then, weak emergency lights clicked on. Within a minute or two, the main lights flickered and then stayed on.

Dan looked over at Ben. His face was ashen and he was perspiring heavily and nearly out of breath.

Clearly embarrassed at his loss of composure, Ben yanked open his paperback with trembling hands and acted as if nothing had happened.

Dan remained silent, though he was tempted to ask Ben why he had panicked. Now curious about the sudden short blackout and sorely in need of a good leg stretch, Dan left his seat and strode in the direction of the main concourse.

He prided himself in being a gym rat and an avid runner, even at age fifty-nine. His workout regimen was a holdover from his NCIS days, but at the root of it was his need to burn off stress. His decades of surviving in a hypercompetitive bureaucracy required him to depend as much on his political skills as it did on subject-matter expertise, and for that he needed a clear head. Exercise helped. As Dan had risen up the career ladder to senior management, he found many who occupied the same perch had done far less and laid claim to far more. His close-cropped hair had long ago turned gray from the never-ending stream of crises, real and imagined, that had to be handled yesterday, and the constant battles with other federal agencies and their people who always thought they were in charge. *No, sir, I won't miss that one bit.*

He'd paid his dues, and now he was enjoying his freedom. *Maybe this retirement gig wasn't so bad after all*, he thought.

His contract job of advising the Defense Department on how their facilities and personnel overseas were vulnerable to terrorist attacks had been easy—his years of dealing with real-world terrorist threats had prepared him well. He felt himself relax.

As Dan picked up his pace, some of his strength returned. He enjoyed the sights and sounds of the increasingly quiet concourse—its growing solitude broken only by an occasional whip of icy rain slapping at the terminal's windows or the whirring sounds of a maintenance worker's floor polisher. The constant beeping of courtesy carts and the frequent gate announcements had long since ceased.

It was nearly seven o'clock and some of those trapped in the airport had already bedded down for the night, in whatever fashion they could.

He passed cluster after cluster of passengers lying on rows of seats. Some stirred restlessly, but most were quietly gazing at smartphones or laptops as others dozed on their makeshift beds on the carpeted floor.

Dan turned the corner and headed down an adjoining concourse; he wanted to get the maximum amount of exercise and check out the rest of the terminal. He gazed forward to gauge the length of the concourse, when something caught his eye. Out of his peripheral vision he saw a lone figure seated on a departure area seat, which caused him to stop. He knew that profile: the dyed black hair and those silver-rimmed glasses—he'd seen it many times.

Dan's stomach tightened as a flood of bad memories came tumbling back into his mind. He held his quick temper in check and remained composed. Stan Crofton was the ultimate backstabber who'd do anything to get ahead. They'd

31

tangled in the field years ago. Crofton's hyper competitiveness bordered on pathology, and over the years he had burned his bridges with almost everyone. Forgetting him was one of the many pleasures Dan had indulged in during retirement. *And now he's back.*

Dan made an immediate U-turn and paced backed down the concourse, fighting his rising anger. He strode directly back to his seat while his mind continued to play back old scenes of conflict and betrayal. As he dropped into his seat he let out a deep breath while he collected his thoughts.

Ben glanced in Dan's direction and acknowledged his return without saying a word. Though relieved to see that Ben's sweating had subsided and his breathing was back to normal, Dan was upset with himself for feeling a renewed sense of rage and a desire for revenge.

As he had done many times on this trip, Dan unzipped his backpack, pulled out a thick book with a plain leather cover, and opened it to a bookmarked page. He wanted to escape into his world of peace.

His reading began to calm him and, after a few minutes, he was able to focus on the passages.

Ben eyed the page Dan was reading, and furrowed his brow. "Didn't peg you as a Bible man. Catholic?" Ben asked in a strained monotone.

Surprised, Dan closed his Bible as if caught in the act of a crime. After sitting speechless for a moment, he answered, "I consider myself a plain ol' Christian. How about you?"

Ben narrowed his eyes. "Let's just say I'm a skeptic." After a lengthy pause, Ben continued. "Actually I'm Jewish, but I haven't been in a synagogue in decades."

*This conversation won't last long,* Dan thought. *I've seen his kind before and I'm not in the mood to spar with some left-wing academic tonight.*

He asked the Lord for peace, and turned to face Ben. "I'm surprised to hear that. I thought most Jews were committed to their faith." The words came out of Dan's mouth before he thought them through.

Ben's laugh was more of a snort. "Not really. Being Jewish is more of an identity—it's a culture. You're born into it and learn to live it. You can be an atheist, but you're still Jewish until death. I'd say about half of all Jews are atheists or agnostics."

Uncomfortable with where the conversation was headed, Dan felt his stress level rising fast. His safe withdrawal from a combative world was being threatened. He had made a point of keeping his faith to himself because he lacked the confidence in his ability to defend his beliefs. That's what his book was all about. He could write it, do the research to back it up, but debate it?

He believed his knowledge level failed to meet the very high standard he held himself to in every other facet of life. He hadn't mastered the facts and details needed to make his case to others as he had in his NCIS profession, where he relished debating points about national security issues with colleagues.

Fighting the urge to get up and move, he clenched his jaw. *Will I ever be ready?* He closed his eyes for an instant, and then took a breath. *It's just another briefing ....*

"So you're an agnostic or an atheist?" Dan asked, looking Ben in the eye.

Ben shrugged. "I don't believe in labels and I don't spend time on subjects that don't interest me. If you don't believe, why waste your time trying to show the other side is wrong? Religion is a business—it's a moneymaking enterprise, and a lot worse in most cases. Not much good has come from man-made religion, and I don't believe in manufactured causes. If you look back through history, you can see that religion has done a lot of damage and killed a lot of people in the name of God."

"I can't argue there. A lot of carnage and mayhem has been committed in the name of organized religion. Christian, Muslim, Jewish, Buddhist, all guilty of being used by man for man's greed and power." Pausing, Dan continued with a puzzled look. "What did you mean by manufactured causes?"

"Look at what man does in the name of 'doing good.' Take the March of Dimes. Their mission was to eradicate polio. They did that in this country, so they no longer had a reason to exist. So what did they do? They took on birth defects as their new cause. No one will ever eliminate birth defects, so they've created their own reason to exist in perpetuity. It's purely business. The church is the same way—at least the Christian religion. Come to us so you don't burn in hell, and oh, by the way, don't forget to write a check! There'll always be a market for people who are scared into buying things. Selling fear works—it's a nice racket."

"Fear is a powerful motivator, I agree. And I'll grant you some charities have a way of self-perpetuating, but some really do help people, and I suspect the March of Dimes does some good. But you're way off on the church being simply fire insurance. The ones that truly base their message on the Bible are at least in part a teaching service—something you should be able to relate to."

"What do you mean?" Ben asked, shifting in his seat to get more comfortable.

"Bible-based churches break down the Scriptures, focus on keys parts, and explain how they relate to life, which is an important part of worship, and worship is the centerpiece of a person's relationship with God. It's hard to have a relationship with someone when you don't know anything about them. That's one of the main reasons for Christian churches to exist—to get the facts out to people who've never studied the Bible or the life of Jesus Christ. You try to do that with your lectures—open the students' eyes to the reality of our world, our culture, and our socially-constructed reality with facts—isn't that right?"

Ben huffed. "Yes, but we base our teachings on empirical evidence. I leave out the mystic philosophy—that's another subject entirely."

"A lot of churches do the same thing. Part of the Bible is eyewitness testimony—sections were written by people who recorded what they observed or learned from firsthand participants. Other parts are prophetic; the predictions made in the Old Testament are borne out in the New Testament."

"Churches are just social clubs."

"That's one element, of course, but they're more than that. They provide a gathering place beyond social interaction—where individuals get instruction, encouragement, and other resources to help them reach out and connect with God—not through the pastors—but with them."

With a deep breath and a barely concealed scowl on his face, Ben spoke with a strained voice. "I take it you've been a big church man your whole life."

"Just the opposite. My parents made me go to church when I was a kid, but I stopped going when I was in high school, and then I drifted further as I got older. My falling away really accelerated while I was in the navy."

"What happened?"

Dan stretched out his long legs and set his Bible on the seat beside him." While I was at sea I got a letter from my home church where I'd been a member since I was about twelve. I hadn't been to church in years, and I didn't know they still carried me on the rolls. Anyway, the letter was accusatory and hostile—it basically said I was going to hell because I'd strayed from the church. Nice way to bring folks back to the fold, right? If I'd been inclined to return to God, that letter would have stopped me in my tracks. What a bunch of hypocrites, I thought. So I spent the next couple of decades living life the way I wanted to. In hindsight, the letter was courageous and exactly what I needed at the time, but I was too busy thinking about myself to recognize it for what it was."

"Sounds like you came to your senses. What got you off track again?" Ben smirked at his own wit.

Dan smiled. "When I remarried, my wife and I started having kids. I felt a sense of obligation to expose my children to the church, and deep down inside, the seeds of my faith were still intact. My parents exposing me to the Christian faith was the best gift they could have ever given me. So I drew on what I sensed to be the right thing to do for my kids' sake, but, to be honest, my heart wasn't in it—at least not in the beginning."

"So what got you to the point of carrying a Bible?"

"It was a gradual process. When we started to take our kids to church out of a sense of obligation, some of the sermons struck a nerve. As I got older, I had this growing feeling that I was missing something in life. The feeling started to get stronger the more successful I became professionally. Looking back, I realize I got fooled into thinking my skills and abilities were all I needed in life. I started to believe all of the walk-on-water performance evaluations I'd gotten and all the plaques and certificates of so-called achievements I hung on my office walls. I became my own little mini-God and my religion was my work. I was financially secure and living the good life, and I had no incentive to seek a higher power that would require me to alter my way of thinking."

"You sound perfectly normal to me. You should embrace your success while you can. There isn't anything else in life."

"I was missing something deep inside. As time went on and I listened to more sermons, I started to take on board some of the themes that touched my soul. I started to figure out there was more to life than material pleasures. I realized why I had an empty feeling."

"Your faith is based on feelings? Isn't that the antithesis of faith? I thought feelings were immaterial to a belief in God—I thought everything was based on an unshakeable faith."

Dan shrugged. "After my kids were older and my professional life stabilized, I had more time to reflect on the meaning of life and death. I'd seen enough of both by that time. I started to devour books about science, history, and archeology. Then I moved on to research about the nature of man's consciousness and the possibility of an afterlife. Not sensational tabloid junk. Serious books and articles written by medical doctors, scientists, and other professionals who had a lot to lose and nothing to gain from promoting their ideas and research. I could see their work actually bolstered the theory that we have immortal souls and that there is a God."

"I don't see how you arrive at a belief in God by buying into the afterlife malarkey."

"I didn't focus just on the generic topic of the afterlife. Some excellent books delve into the historical and archeological evidence of the life of Christ and his ministry of miracles."

Ben laughed heartily. "So you were really a feel-good Christian in search of evidence to support your faith."

"I wasn't a true Christian when I started to read books about consciousness and the soul. It started me on the path I'm on now. They interested me—first, from a curiosity standpoint, and then from the standpoint that I was looking at evidence. Now I'm working on a book of my own, for people like me. People who don't understand their faith, but have one."

Ben looked impressed. "You're writing a book? From spook to scholar, eh?"

Dan joined Ben in a good-natured laugh. "Something like that," he replied.

"Well, when you get it written, you let me know. It might make a good case study for one of my sociology classes someday."

Dan relaxed in the seat and closed his eyes. "I'll do that, Ben Chernick. But right now, I've got to rest these tired eyes."

"Can we talk more later?" Ben asked.

Dan gave a faint smile with his eyes closed. "Sure, Ben," he said. "Whatever you need."

# CHAPTER FOUR

## *Opening the Case*

"Bet they'll have a closed casket for that one," quipped one of the firemen standing near the crash site.

A police officer nodded as he dug through the wet mixture of foam, ash, and incinerated metal pieces to search for clues about the driver who'd been transported to the medical examiner's office a few minutes earlier. However, a fellow officer had already removed the driver's wallet sometime earlier in the evening.

The surges of electrical current from the downed transmission lines had partially melted the VIN number on the tanker and, for the time being, the Charlotte-Mecklenburg Police Department was treating the victim as a John Doe pending the identification of the truck's owner. The substation was completely shut down, causing rolling blackouts in the area as the grid struggled to meet demand.

A short distance away, the emergency generators at Charlotte Douglas Airport labored to keep electrical power flowing into the expansive terminal.

\*\*\*

Adding to the lingering effects of his acrimonious debate with Ben and his near encounter with Stan Crofton, Dan had a feeling of unease he couldn't shake. He took off on another hike through the glass-and-steel jungle he was trapped in, looking for a private area to make a call home. He spotted a gate waiting area that was nearly deserted. He dropped into a seat in the corner by the window and hit the speed dial.

"Connie? Hon, it's me. You there?" he asked the answering machine that had picked up on the fourth ring." Hon, I need to talk to you … you there?" He waited a long moment.

His reward was her sweet voice on the line. "Hello?" she mumbled.

"I'm sorry, honey. I woke you …."

She laughed, and he felt peace begin to replace his irritation.

She said, "Not a problem, worrywart. I was hoping you'd call. Looks like I fell asleep in the chair. I can't get up as fast as I once did. Are you doing all right? I heard the weather is awful up there."

"It is pretty ugly, that's the truth. We're trapped here at this point, but at least we're indoors, the heat and lights are still on, though barely, at times. Been in worse spots, but still I wanted to be home by now. With you."

"I know. I wanted that too. You've been away too long. But you stay safe and be on the next flight home. I'll be here. Any word on when the next flight might be?"

"Last we heard, it will be in the morning. They said at seven."

"Something wrong, Dan? You sound preoccupied."

"I am. You'll never guess who I saw a few minutes ago, right in this airport."

She was quiet a moment. "Sorry, I can't imagine …."

He rubbed a hand over his face as though to wipe away the anger rising in his chest again.

"Hon?" she prompted.

"As sure as I'm talking with you, I saw Stan Crofton sitting in a gate area. Can't believe it. All these miles, all these years, and there he is. And I'm pissed off all over again."

She sighed. "I'm sorry, Dan. But you know how God works in us. He'll keep putting us in places to face the things we need to learn from, right? If you're still angry with Stan, then maybe you need to pray again about forgiving him. There's no excuse for what he did, but for your sake, you need to clean this out."

Dan took a deep breath as the lights flickered. He nodded. "You're right, as always. Connie, I really needed to hear your voice. I'll let you go. I'm going to head back to my seat and see if I can get some sleep."

"Like that's going to happen," she said with a smile in her voice. "You stay safe, my guardian angel, okay? I love you. Keep me posted on the flights so I can pick you up."

After they said good-bye, he tucked his phone away and flexed his tired shoulders. Connie was right. He thought he'd forgiven Stan, but apparently not completely. He'd moved on. He'd put it behind him—but that wasn't the same thing, was it?

The normally busy terminal corridors were now nearly deserted. As Dan made his way back to his gate, he scanned the shops and eateries for a place still open. Although it was past 9:00 p.m., a few of the stores remained open to take advantage of the captive potential customers.

\*\*\*

Dan returned to his seat and set his heavy backpack on the floor. He had never let it out of his sight the entire month-long trip, but then, by this stage in his career he'd developed operational security habits that were second nature to him. His years of staying one step ahead of hostile intelligence services had ingrained in him the need to protect his laptop.

He noted the tattered paperback on Ben's empty seat. *Gone for a smoke, no doubt ....*

Dan sighed and let the fatigue settle in. He positioned the backpack to work as a pillow, rested his head, and closed his eyes.

\*\*\*

"We're *definitely* not going anywhere tonight."

Ben's loud pronouncement roused Dan out of a shallow sleep. Dan looked at his watch and realized he'd been dozing for nearly a half hour. Only nine thirty? He swallowed a groan. "That's what they've been saying." He yawned.

Ben said, "The roads are a sheet of glass and sidewalks are like an ice skating rink. I almost slipped and broke my neck. But that would be a lot quicker than gradually smoking myself to death, I suppose."

Ben's sudden weight on the row of seats jarred Dan into a sitting position. As he cleared his head, Dan tried to read Ben's face. From the side, he couldn't see Ben's trademark smirk.

Dan answered, "That's a pretty fatalistic attitude to take, my friend. If you know smoking's so bad for you, why don't you quit?"

Ben cleared his throat as he shook his head and momentarily closed his eyes. "I wish it was that easy. When you have an addictive personality like I do, breaking old habits is hard—"

He lapsed into a deep cough that morphed into wheezing and creaking sounds in his chest. While gasping for air, he reached into his blazer and pulled out an inhaler. After spraying a couple of shots into his mouth, he eased his head back, closed his eyes, and held his breath. Then he started to take in some deep breaths. Dan watched Ben's chest heave at an increasingly slower pace, until his breathing became more normal.

"Emphysema," Ben rasped. "I've had it for years. The doctors warned me that my smoking would be fatal, but I'm still here. That's one of the reasons my daughter and I had a falling out. She wanted me to quit and I told her to mind her own business. I guess she got tired of taking me to the emergency room in the middle of the night. She's pretty hardheaded and won't take no for an answer—like her old man."

"Is that why you haven't visited her?"

"No, that's not the reason. She made a very unfortunate choice for a husband, and I was candid with her about her error in judgment."

Dan laughed softly. Ben was quite the character. "Did you ever meet him?"

"Once." Ben nodded. "Ruth brought him home for dinner after they started dating. I saw enough right then to know she was making a mistake. She wouldn't listen, and pursued the relationship anyway. They got married about a year later at his church, but I refused to go. I didn't want to be a party to my daughter ruining her life. That pretty much sealed my fate. She wouldn't talk to me after that."

"That sounds extreme. What was so bad about him?"

"Well, first of all, he isn't a Jew. Secondly, he's a mechanic or something, and Ruth has a doctorate in Asian studies. Total mismatch. I warned her she was making a mistake, but she dug in her heels—like her mother. You have to have common interests and a compatible background, and even then there are no guarantees. She wouldn't listen, and took it personally. Our rift started when I divorced her mother and then her wedding was the final straw. She blamed me for the divorce."

"So how long have they been married?" Dan asked.

"I think about fifteen years."

Dan laughed louder than he'd intended in the quiet terminal. "So much for the mismatch."

Ben scowled. "Give 'em time. She'll outgrow him."

"Sounds like they're doing okay to me. Does her husband have any sort of religious faith? You said they were married in a church."

"He's a Protestant; I don't remember the specific denomination."

"If he'd been Jewish, would that have made a difference?"

"In my day, Jews didn't aspire to blue-collar jobs or manual labor. I grant you, my father was in the garment business, but I was expected to surpass his station in life. We're defined by our profession—a proper Jew is expected to get a graduate-level education and become an accomplished professional—a doctor, a lawyer, or even a professor. Like I said, it's cultural. If he'd been a Jew, I would have probably overlooked his lack of achievement, but since he wasn't, it was a moot point."

Ben paused and stared at the floor. "Sounds extreme," he confided, "but in my world if you're not a Jew, you're a heathen. Period. I know it's nonsense, but it's reflexive— burned into the psyche as a kid growing up in a Jewish family. It's also pride and arrogance, and a defense mechanism."

He lowered his voice and looked directly at Dan. "It's ironic. For an ethnic group that was nearly exterminated by other groups for being impure, we practice our own form of benign bigotry. We don't discuss it openly, but we live it."

"Sounds like you've got some major repair work to do with your daughter and her husband."

"I know," Ben answered, looking away from Dan.

"So, you're divorced? How long?" Dan asked.

"It's been a while. I guess you could say I'm hard to live with. I'm very outspoken and very opinionated—in case you haven't noticed. It comes with the territory; it's a hazard of higher education. Plus, there were other issues."

Dan was regretting that he'd asked. He could tell Ben had more to say, but he was so tired he wasn't sure he wanted to hear it. Despite that, he replied, "I see."

"I had an affair." Ben gazed at the floor and said, "I don't know why I'm talking about this, but it doesn't matter, I guess. She was a graduate student who worked for me at the time. She was beautiful, and I seduced her. A huge taboo in those days, but we kept it discreet. Or, so I thought. My wife found out and confronted me one day. In my typically arrogant fashion, I told her it was none of her business and she knew where the door was if she wanted to use it. Big mistake when your wife's a lawyer. She took me literally and walked out. I'm still paying for that mistake today."

Dan was beginning to see a vulnerable, broken man under Ben's gruff exterior of feigned intellectual superiority. Ben was now lost in his own thoughts as he vocalized the mental pictures flashing through his mind, so Dan stayed quiet and listened.

"After the lovely student ran off and my wife left me, I realized I was married to my career. The teaching and the research—they had become my life. I had no existence outside of the classroom, my office, and my library at home. My lectures, my 'learned opinions,' and the few times I was published defined me."

Dan could understand the tunnel vision. It was a valid hazard. He nodded. "I think a lot of people end up married to their career. ... How long have you been divorced?"

"Sixteen years." Still staring at the floor, Ben continued. "You can lose yourself in your ideas—in a sort of theoretical world. You see everything as patterns and cause and effect. I guess that's what happened with my wife and my daughter. I deluded myself into thinking I didn't need them. I stopped thinking of them as human beings. I stopped thinking of myself as a human being."

"At least you realize the mistakes you've made and now you're correcting your errors," Dan offered. He shifted in the seat so he could see Ben better.

"Not all of them. The emphysema has slowed me down, but I still can't stop smoking. I suppose if I don't stop, I'll die—maybe soon. Not a bad thing, actually. I've made quite a mess of things."

Ben peeled off his blazer and settled back in his seat as his breathing became less labored.

"How about you? Did you ever smoke?" Ben asked.

"Nah, I tried it when I was a kid, but didn't like it. Nobody in my family smokes."

Ben turned to Dan and looked at him as if he had finally accepted him as a peer. "You said you're married?"

"Yep, twenty-nine years. I was lucky to find a good woman, and I guess I was too busy working to completely screw it up."

"You're a rare breed. Twenty-nine years is a record these days. I don't know of many couples who've lasted that long. Didn't you say you'd been married before?"

"I did. I married my girlfriend right before I went in the navy, but it didn't last. One day I got a Dear John letter. I'd been expecting it because I suspected all along she was seeing someone else while I was gone. But it still hit me hard. We began the divorce process when I came home on leave a year later. That started my moral decay."

"Well," Ben said, "sounds like you woke up and decided to smell the roses. Nothing wrong with living in the present, Dan."

"The present without God is not the way I want to live today, but I get your point." After a pause, Dan continued. "Speaking of the present, must still be tough being a professor with all those young coeds in front of you every day."

"You get used to it. At my age, you become numb to what used to bring you pleasure. I suppose it's a stage in my life, but to be frank, I hope it passes. How about you? I'm sure you've been tempted in your profession." Ben lowered his face and peered at Dan with a look of anticipation.

"I think most people in my business are tempted at some point in their career. It's just how you handle it."

"So you never caved to your baser instincts?" Ben asked.

Dan shook his head, and almost laughed at Ben's look of disappointment. "I had the advantage early on of being afraid of losing my job. And I loved Connie—I wasn't willing to hurt her like I'd been hurt. But in the job, I had nothing to fall back on. We were always under the microscope from the day we were hired and always in fear of someone making a complaint or calling in to report something we did. Because we dealt with the darker side of life, you couldn't help but be exposed to temptations. But fortunately, our methods of operation had a few safeguards built in."

"You know, academia has rules too. We break them."

"True enough, but for example, we couldn't interview a female in an interrogation room alone. We always needed a second agent as a witness. Ditto if we were going to transport a female in a government car; we needed a second agent to ride along."

"That sounds reasonable."

"We always had to be on guard because the bad guys and even our friends threw traps in our way. Usually, though, we did it to ourselves," Dan said. "You saw what happened to the Secret Service agents in Colombia with the prostitutes, right? Eventually, everyone talks to someone. Sometimes the threat came at us in a more subtle way. We had to be alert and in control at all times, which is hard to do."

"What sorts of threats did you face?"

"Let's say I have seen temptation up close and personal—and the consequences, too. In my case, my fear of the consequences kept me on the straight and narrow."

Ben's laugh was gruff. "I knew the consequences, but figured I was willing to pay the price if necessary."

"I'm not speaking about losing my job or my wife, Ben. I was handling sources who could have had me killed if I crossed the wrong one by messing with his lady. I had more than one source whose mistress hit on me. In every case, I was clear I wasn't interested. Sometimes the situations got dicey."

"Interesting. Did it happen a lot?"

"Yeah, a few times, but fortunately I was able to stay in control. Like I said, I'm no saint, but by the grace of God I was able to keep my nose clean and do my job."

"I notice you leave out a lot of details in your stories. Does that come from your training?"

"I learned early on to be discreet and not discuss details—particularly when they deal with anything that touches on a sensitive area. Talking about foreign officials and confidential sources and the like, even years later, is not the sort of information I'm going to discuss in public. You never know when it will come back to bite you."

Ben shifted in his seat, cocked his head, and gaped at Dan with a curious expression. He said, "You strike me as a rational person to have had the career you did, but I still can't understand how you could buy into the Bible myth."

"Well, fella," Dan said, peering at his watch while rubbing his sore eyes, "we've got time, if you want to hear the tale."

# CHAPTER FIVE

## *Patterns*

"It was my reading that got me started," Dan said, putting his backpack on the floor between his feet and stretching his legs. "The information is out there for anyone who's interested, but you have to be willing to dig through some pretty dry material and sift out the bogus information. Initially I focused on the claims about the unique qualities of the Bible itself—the very power of the words."

"You make it sound like it's a book of magic."

"You're not far off, Ben. It's a self-authenticating document."

"Now, that's a new one."

Dan noted Ben's incredulous look, and went on. "I always pictured the Bible as a musty old collection of archaic stories that bordered on mythology. Then I discovered some work by a man by the name of Dr. Ivan Panin, a Russian immigrant who was a master literary critic and also an agnostic who converted to Christianity. He discovered that the Bible was written in mathematical patterns. Both the Hebrew and the Greek translations are constructed in sentences and verses that are all multiples of seven. I was amazed to find out the entire

Bible is written that way. No other literary work on the planet has the mathematical patterns of the Bible."

"Mathematical patterns?"

"Yeah, both Hebrew and Greek letters also have numeric values, and, using those values to do precise calculations, he went through the entire original Hebrew texts of the Old Testament and the Greek texts of the New Testament and found they are written in specific numeric patterns that are present in every part—and I mean the entire Bible. It's written with words and sentence structures all divisible by the number seven. For example, according to Panin, the numeric value of the Greek vocabulary words in the second chapter of Mark is exactly 161, or twenty-three sevens. The number of Greek letters in those 161 words is divisible by seven, and the numeric value of the 161 words is also divisible by seven. The whole Bible is full of patterns of letters, words, phrases, and chapter features divisible by seven. The probability of that happening by accident is virtually zero. That got my attention. I started to look at the Bible in an entirely different light after that." He stopped there to gauge Ben's reaction.

"I've never heard of the man."

"I hadn't either, but after I read about his work—which took about fifty years of his life—I looked for other researchers who also corroborated that the Bible contained numeric patterns and numerically repetitive symbolism. For example, others have pointed out that Jesus told seven parables during his time on earth and he spoke seven times while on the cross. The letters of the word cross, written in Hebrew, add up to 777. Seven is the number of completion. Eight is the number of resurrection and renewal and also of Jesus Christ. All of the names of our Messiah in the Bible are multiples of eight. Likewise with Satan—all of his names are multiples of 13, and the numbers of the name Antichrist add up to 666. I don't think it's an accident or mere chance.

"After I realized the assertions about the numeric patterns in the Bible were mathematically provable, I started looking at other parts of the Bible that set it apart from any other written work in history. I'll give you an example. There's a verse in the Book of Isaiah which was written in the seventh or eighth century BC. It describes the Earth as a circle. How did the writer know? The Bible also has more than sixty prophecies about Jesus Christ, and every one of them came true hundreds of years later. How do you explain that? You can't. One scientist calculated that the odds of just eight of the Messianic prophecies in the Bible about the birth, life, and death of Jesus Christ all actually occurring, as one in 10 to the 17th power."

Ben said quickly, "That's been published?"

"It has. Dr. Peter Stoner wrote his book in 1958, and it was peer reviewed. Once I started to understand that the Bible contained truly supernatural content, I began to dig through parts that I thought were merely symbolism, like the Book of Genesis. I started to reread the Bible and treat the accounts as literal, like the description of creation. Dr. Henry Morris has done some outstanding work on the creation account of Genesis, through an analysis of geology and the Scriptures. I also looked at articles about the structure of cells, and later on I did a lot of reading about history, astronomy, and archeology. Most people wouldn't touch the stuff, but I found some nuggets of information that intrigued me."

"You must have been really bored," Ben commented. "I get paid to read professional journals, and I can't say I'd be tempted to dwell on the finer points of cellular structure."

"What I read surprised me, Ben. While I was in school in the '50s and '60s, I was exposed to a lot of so-called discoveries claiming that evolution explained how man arrived on earth. Everything from *Life* magazine and the *National Geographic*, to lectures later on while I was in college during the '70s. I never questioned the validity of the theory, and even though I was sort of a closet Christian, I somehow reconciled the conflict between the account of creation of man in the Bible and the supposed clear science of evolution as, somehow, a matter of semantics. I convinced myself that the Bible contained metaphorical language, and evolution made a more precise description in modern terms of how life progressed on earth."

"Evolution is science." Ben's tone had returned to an agitated monotone.

"I disagree. It's a philosophical theory and nothing more. I was surprised to find there are more holes in evolution than a piece of Swiss cheese, and that was what got me going. I was shocked that none of the problems with evolution were ever discussed when I went to school. I know science was not nearly as advanced in those days, but even now, you never hear of all the gaps and discrepancies in the evolutionary theory. When someone does bring up a problem with evolution, they're ridiculed and marginalized."

"You're not a biologist or a geologist. You don't have the academic background to critique scientific theories."

"No, but I have the background to critique human sources of information, and since Darwin is considered the father of evolution, there was a lot there for me to look at."

"A lot more scientists than Darwin supported evolution in the early years," Ben said. "He's just the most familiar name to the public."

"Let's face it, almost everyone associates Darwin with the development of evolutionary theory, so he's the one I focused on. I essentially did what I would have done if I was still in my old job—I vetted a source."

"What does Darwin's background have to do with the existence of God?"

"A lot! What was his motivation for his development of the theory of natural selection? Was he really simply an objective scientist who reported the results of his scientific studies in a neutral way, or did he have an atheistic agenda? A person's mindset can have a major bearing on the truthfulness of any information they report. It guides them to embellish, hold back, fabricate, or be totally truthful. That's one of the areas we focus on when we vet and validate sources."

Ben argued, "Most people don't care about his background, just the results of his work. He used sound scientific methods to produce evidence to support his work, and that's more than you can do to prove the existence of your God!"

"I thought so too. And then I found out Darwin didn't have any type of degree in science. He'd been in medical school, but he dropped out and studied divinity at Christ's College at the University of Cambridge. When he made his infamous voyage on the *HMS Beagle* to South America, he had no scientific credentials of any kind, and he was young and inexperienced to boot. But what was more revealing to me was that Darwin was undergoing a crisis in his faith. He had read a book about geology that attacked, indirectly, creationism, and his superficial faith began to crumble. Then he made a conscious and deceptive turn to refute the writings about intelligent design, rather than report the findings of his alleged scientific inquiries. He began to descend into atheistic beliefs, but he hid them because they weren't politically correct at the time."

Dan straightened his body and said, "Some think his real motive for writing *On the Origin of Species* was to question the existence of God and his act of creation. I believe he ultimately started the rift between science and Christianity that exits today. He had an agenda that he hid, and that made him suspect in my mind."

"So what? That doesn't disprove his findings," Ben stated with a defiant tone.

"But motives influence actions and color judgment. And what kind of individual produced those alleged findings? A person with irreconcilable internal conflicts that caused chronic depression, panic attacks, and a lot of psychosomatic illnesses. We're supposed to accept the results of his work as the product of a rational mind seeking objective facts? Not me. He produced almost no scientific facts—only assumptions that were the product of a manipulative, mentally-ill mind. Had he been honest about his true beliefs at the time in Victorian Europe, his books would have never seen the light of day, and you and I wouldn't have received the indoctrination we did in American public schools in the '60s and later."

Ben said, "He was sane enough to write an impressive book. So what if he had some mental health issues? We all do."

"It calls into question his theories and how he arrived at them. Like I said, in my business, we evaluate the *source* of information when we attempt to make a judgment about the veracity and accuracy of the information. Darwin was deceptive and that would make me wary about accepting anything he had to report."

"You keep saying Darwin didn't produce any evidence to back up his theories, but you haven't either."

"That's not true. You use the term 'evidence.' In my business there are different kinds of evidence. We often build cases on circumstantial evidence. A murderer usually doesn't make a video of his crime and then conveniently leave a copy with the prosecutor on the way home. He instinctively tries to conceal what he did, but we're able to use advanced investigative techniques to piece together clues—physical evidence—of a person's acts when he or she committed a crime. People are convicted for murder when the body of the victim has never been recovered."

"But Dan, somebody with your background doesn't impress me as someone who'd believe in myths and superstition."

"You know people in my business are mostly hardened skeptics. We don't take anyone or anything at face value. And you're right, CI people are the most wary and suspicious group of all. We tend to see the worst in people and believe almost nothing unless we've checked it out ourselves. We don't trust people, so, yes, we aren't prone to believe in stories or what someone says, who comes in off the street."

Ben narrowed his eyes as he listened.

"I'll go even further. In the CI business, we don't believe in coincidences. Some of us made a living out of performing clandestine acts in public areas without anyone noticing—doing things that appear to be normal, but in reality were part of a carefully planned and choreographed operation. The public goes about its business, shrugging off something that may look a little odd … like a person bending down and making a mark on a wall or dropping a piece of what appears to be trash along a back road. Most people tend to rationalize and explain away little inconsistencies that appear around them. Those of us in the CI world look for those same acts to catch spies. We know the enemy counts on people responding in a predictable way."

"So what's your point?"

"Scientists are deliberately ignoring signs of the existence of God because many in the scientific community have tied their careers to the theory of evolution. They have a vested interest in dismissing or depressing any evidence that could debunk the theory. It's a matter of self-preservation."

"Even if you're correct, that doesn't advance your belief that God exists."

Dan shot back with a calm but forceful response. "If you can destroy the authenticity of the Bible, you can turn people away from God. The theory of evolution is a direct frontal assault on the Bible and, by extension, God. But if you can expose major flaws in evolution, then some may seek answers that can only be found in the Bible."

Ben said, "So you really think there's a grand conspiracy to prop up the theory of evolution and dismiss contradictory evidence? How's that possible?"

"I don't think there's a grand conspiracy," Dan said, shaking his head. "But I do think there's groupthink in many academic and scientific circles in America and Europe today, and it started over a century ago. Those who subscribe to the groupthink are rewarded socially and financially with better opportunities in the scientific and academic worlds."

"Groupthink?" Ben asked with a frown.

"Yeah. I think the roots of groupthink about evolution began in the 1800s, when American academics seeking graduate-level degrees were forced to go to European universities because American colleges didn't offer them at that time. Many European academics were already liberal and bent toward atheism. American scholars were infected with a liberal bias and an anti-God posture, and they brought that line of thinking back to the U.S. Once our institutions of higher learning were infected, many fields of study were affected. After Darwin dispersed the seeds of his theory of natural selection, they found fertile ground in American academics over time. They became almost impossible to dig out and expose once they took root. When I sat in class, I never once got a hint that any of the theory of evolution was in any way potentially wrong, and I'm sure it's the same way today."

"Give me an example of a hole in evolutionary theory." Ben crossed his arms and looked away from Dan.

"I'll use Darwin's own words to demonstrate his theory is wrong. He essentially stated that if someone could demonstrate that a complex organism that existed in the present day didn't undergo numerous, successive, slight modifications over time, then his theory would break down."

"And what would be the example of that?"

"The fossils found in layers of rock from the Cambrian Period. There's clear evidence of an unexplained explosion of complex life-forms that appeared out of nowhere. There are no fossils of precursor organisms that led to all of the animal and plant forms."

"I don't know the details of the controversy, but I suspect there's a logical explanation."

"I haven't found one. If viable complex life-forms come from slow, successive, random mutations of organisms over time, then there should have been a fossil record of the earlier life-forms. Of course, another explanation is that a massive worldwide flood deposited plant and animal life all over the planet in a matter of weeks, including marine life on the tops of mountains. Hence, the rich layer of fossils in a relatively thin layer of sediment in the earth's crust."

Ben said, "I'm confident scientists will find an answer to the Cambrian question, and then your argument will collapse. And as far as your flood theory goes, spare me the fairy tales. Have any other examples?"

"I do. One example is the bat. Fossils of bats that are allegedly over twenty million years old have been found, and the bats are almost exactly the same as they are today. No fossils of precursor species of ground-dwelling, bat-like animals have ever been found; bats just appeared."

"That's your evidence? No missing link for a bat?"

"Oh, that's one of many. Another is the nautilus. The ones you find today are nearly the same as the ones found fossilized from long ago. Why didn't they evolve? Where are the fossils of the earlier species?"

"That doesn't mean the fossils don't exist; it means they haven't been found yet. Besides, they're weak examples. We know from fossils, that animals have evolved over many millions of years. Look at dinosaurs. Their fossils are everywhere. We know they died off long ago, after a cataclysmic event, and more advanced life-forms appeared in their place. A lot has to do with where they died and how their fossils have been preserved."

"Actually, Ben, you just gave an example that helps cast into doubt one of the foundational elements of the theory of evolution, but I bet you weren't even aware of what's been found."

"All right, enlighten me."

"Some of the fossilized dinosaur bones that have been discovered contain soft tissue, blood vessels, and connective tissue. Can soft tissue survive for sixty or seventy million years without complete decomposition? That's a legitimate question no one can prove one way or the other. Some scientists estimate that soft tissue could survive for maybe five or six million years at most, if completely frozen."

Ben smiled. "I've never heard that."

"It's true, but it's not getting wide exposure in evolution circles," Dan explained, his fatigue falling away to a new focus. "Evolution is partially based on the premise that life on earth evolved over hundreds of millions of years, yet we now have physical evidence that suggests dinosaurs roamed the earth only five or six thousand years ago, or even earlier. One explanation you hear today is that the iron in the dinosaurs' body somehow prevented decomposition. Others flatly state that our understanding of decomposition is now wrong."

"There must be some explanation for the dinosaurs' soft tissue," argued Ben. "Maybe the fossils were formed in perfectly airtight pockets that preserved the material. We'll probably never know, since the geological processes involved in forming fossils took millions of years to complete."

"You've touched on another area where recent findings have shattered assumptions about the geological processes associated with evolution and the possible age of the earth."

"And what might that be?"

"How long do you think it took to form the Grand Canyon?"

"I don't know. Maybe … at least a hundred million years or more. I'm not a geologist, but I'd say, based on the depth of the canyon, it had to take at least 50 million years for the river to erode it to the depth that it's at today."

"Do you believe it could have been made in less than a month?"

"You're not serious!"

"I am. Remember Mount St. Helens?"

"Who could forget? Utter devastation."

"And the devastation resulted in the creation of a canyon over one thousand feet wide and one hundred forty feet deep, with a river at the bottom, in one day. It also resulted in the deposit of many hundreds of layers of fine sediment in the canyon walls during the same brief period. The layers look like they were deposited over hundreds of centuries or longer. Powerful natural events like a volcanic explosion or a massive flood can force geological changes that appear to have taken much longer."

"It's the first I've heard of that, but I still think Darwin's work has stood the test of time."

"It's stood the test of time because it has been *protected*, not challenged. Had electron microscopes been in existence during Darwin's day, I think we'd be studying something different in school today. Had Darwin been aware of the complexity of the process needed to make proteins from amino acids, he would have probably shelved his whole theory."

"Now you're speculating."

"I'm stating a strong hypothesis. You know proteins are the building blocks of living organisms. The process needed to create different proteins is so complex and intricate that the odds against it occurring by chance are off the charts. But you know it goes beyond that. Even if you conceded that RNA and DNA could somehow self-assemble by random mutations—which I don't believe could happen—you still can't account for the appearance of complex body plans that appeared in the so-called Cambrian age. No amount of genetic mutations could cause the complex animals that suddenly appeared."

"Now you're stating an opinion."

"I'm stating evidence backed by statistical probability. No one knows how a fertilized egg can divide into specialized cells that produce specific parts of an organism like the skeletal structure, the gut, and the eyes. No mutations of RNA and DNA can account for the unique biological commands resident in cells of a fertilized egg. Those commands sure look like execution orders that follow a specific blueprint. Blueprints come from intelligent sources that have specific outcomes in mind. No mere series of genetic accidents could account for the wide variety of blueprints that cells contain. Evolutionists have no answers."

"Science always comes up with the answers eventually. Maybe not in our lifetimes, but it will. We have to be patient."

Dan said, "We've been waiting for over a hundred and fifty years to find the answers to the problems that plague

Darwin's theory. I think the exact opposite is happening. As the complexity of even the simplest life-forms becomes more evident, evolution continues to collapse under the weight of its own archaic principles. More and more, some scientists are starting to realize there is an elegant sophistication to life, and that can only come from an intelligent source that we can't detect—a supernatural creator."

"We're back to magic and superstition, are we?"

"Not magic, Ben. Processes that we can't identify or detect with any of today's technology, and the one term that fits is 'supernatural.' We see events that are clearly supernatural in origin, but we don't recognize them for what they are. For example, we hear about people who are miraculously cured of advanced terminal illnesses. Spontaneous remission—really? Explain that in scientific terms. We see events around us that have no explanation, but we shrug them off as anomalies. We should be studying such incredible events and carefully documenting them. We hear that there is no evidence of God on earth, but I say there are forms of evidence appearing all around us all the time."

"I don't believe in miracles, but I get your point." Ben paused. "I'm still waiting to hear about some real evidence of your God's existence."

"The evidence becomes obvious when you study Darwin's work. A number of people have pointed out the ultimate flaw in his theory—a flaw that leads us in one direction."

"Back to Darwin, are we? I thought we put him to bed."

Dan laughed. "Wish I was put to bed at this point." He shook his head. "The biggest hole in Darwin's theory is he can't account for the origin of life. His theory picks up midstream when life is already on earth, and postulates how it progressed and evolved through random changes."

"What's wrong with that?" Ben asked.

"It ignores the fundamental question that has to be answered before jumping to conclusions about how life advanced. You know the law of biogenesis: life must come from life—it can't be created from nonliving matter. Yet it gets pushed to the side when evolution is discussed. If you can create reasonable doubt about the ability of life to self-generate, then you also cast into serious doubt the follow-on theories about how the process of established life-forms evolved on their own. The whole direction in which Darwin tries to lead science becomes a dead end."

"I'm sure there are explanations."

"There are, but if you look at how the evolution crowd postulates about how life began, you realize how shaky the whole theoretical package is."

"I suppose you have more quote, evidence, unquote?"

"I do. When you look at the theories about basic life-forms self-assembled out of the raw materials on the earth, you find insurmountable problems. I'm not a biologist, but I understand that researchers have determined even the most basic components of cells are highly complex. They all have precise biochemical structures that must be present for the cell to live. If one element of a cell is not in the proper location, the cell can't function. Isn't that correct?"

Ben nodded.

Dan went on. "When people realize how extremely intricate cellular structures are, and then start to ask questions about how such a complicated structure could self-assemble and then self-replicate in the very unstable primitive environment of earth, you have to ask the question: How did it all start in the beginning? A prominent scientist has made this compelling case: Some biological systems are so complex that unless all of the indispensable parts are present in the system at once, the system could never function, even in a reduced capacity. In other words, the system would have to appear already assembled since it couldn't function in a partially assembled mode. He called his theory 'irreducible complexity.' I think it's a powerful concept that holds water."

"Science is an ongoing process and discoveries come to light over time," Ben stated. "Besides, if I recall correctly, the irreducible complexity theory has been be debunked."

"Debunked is the wrong term," Dan replied. "I think 'ineffectively challenged' is the more correct way to describe the response from certain evolutionists. They claim that the irreducible complexity theory is fatally flawed because indirect evolutionary pathways to some complex biological systems are possible. Almost anything is possible, so their response, in my opinion, is very weak. I believe the correct question is: Are the evolutionary pathways really scientifically plausible? In other words, are the odds of their occurring by chance within reason, or off the charts? In the case of some systems, I believe the answer is off the charts."

"I think with enough time, any biological system can self-assemble from raw materials."

"I doubt it," Dan said, shaking his head. "Take, for example, the flagellum of bacteria, the tiny little rotor mechanism that propels the bacteria around. It looks like a tail under a microscope. When I saw its intricate construction, I was amazed. It's like a microscopic outboard motor. I'm not a microbiologist, but speaking as someone who likes to tinker with engines, I'm convinced that something so complex could not put itself together by chance. If it couldn't assemble itself, then bacteria would have no method of moving and it couldn't survive. Evolution has no viable answers. Like I said, if advanced microscopes had existed during Darwin's life, his theory would have been dead on arrival."

"No one will ever know how life really began," Ben announced caustically.

"I think we know the answer." Dan held up his Bible and looked straight at Ben. "Whether we want to admit that or not."

# CHAPTER SIX

## *Old Becomes New*

"What!" yelled Ben, causing Dan to jump in his seat. Ben turned his back on Dan to listen.

"Yeah," the caller said, "we dodged a bullet. Carson Hall took a direct hit, but the Davis Center got nicked with some minor damage—looks like mostly broken windows."

"Where are you?" Ben asked in a whisper.

"I'm slogging around the quad. What a mess. Cops and fire trucks everywhere. It looks like a war zone here."

Adam, Ben's graduate assistant, gave a running account of the disaster scene. "You're not gonna believe this," Adam blurted out. "A tree trunk went right through the top floor and missed your office by about fifty feet. I don't think there's any damage to your spaces, but I won't know for sure until I can get inside and have a look."

Adam's voice was tinged with disbelief. "The roof's still on and only a few windows were broken, but none of yours. This whole place is a mess, though—pieces of trees and buildings everywhere. I'm gonna try to sneak in and take a peek before security gets here."

Ben clasped his phone tightly as he listened to Adam's description of the damage. He cut his gaze in Dan's direction, then got to his feet and moved away. He longed for a cigarette.

"Check my safe, and don't get caught! It's behind the double doors of my credenza, next to my desk. Make sure you find it!" Ben said, raising his voice. He paced back toward the window.

Dan looked at Ben with a quizzical look.

Ben covered the phone and whispered in Dan's direction: "A tornado hit the college—our buildings. A lot of damage. I keep some important personal items in my office." Ben looked away as his words tailed off.

"Sure hope everything's okay," answered Dan. He closed his eyes and leaned his head back against the seat.

Ben needed to focus on the call. He'd deal with Dan's questions later.

"Okay, okay, thanks for keeping me posted, and call me as soon you know—day or night."

He slipped the phone into his jacket pocket and scrubbed his hands over his face. How long since he'd had any energy at all? Joy? He gulped a deep breath, fought the urge to cough, and dropped heavily onto his seat.

"This storm's much larger than we thought. My campus is hundreds of miles from here and we got hit."

"Are you still gonna see your daughter?" Dan asked, without opening his eyes.

"Yeah. There's no sense in rushing home now. My grad assistant will keep me posted. Doesn't sound like my office was damaged at all, but it'll take months to get most of the campus put back together."

"There was a lot of other damage?" Dan asked, sitting up to look at Ben.

"Sounds like our History Department took a direct hit. It's in Carson Hall, and from what Adam said, the building is essentially gone."

"That's too bad. I liked modern history when I was in college, but my reading lately has also gotten me interested in ancient history."

"We have a fairly large History Department—most liberal arts schools do."

"I don't suppose your university offers any biblical history courses?"

"No, thank goodness. We have good academic credentials, and I'd hate to see them tarnished by some amped-up Sunday school classes—wouldn't be good for our reputation."

Dan laughed. "I think the study of the historical facts about the places and people described in the Bible would be of great interest. Almost all reputable historians acknowledge the existence and life of Christ, as well as many of the events and people mentioned in the Bible."

"Oh, really?" Ben settled back in his seat, relieved that Dan was back on his case about proving God was real. *Much safer topic for me, actually.* He even smiled a little. But he was so tired ....

"When Christ was on the cross, the entire world went dark even though it was midday," Dan began. "The Greek historian Thallus wrote about a well-known event of noontime darkness that occurred during his lifetime, and it coincided with the crucifixion. Thallus' explanation was that darkness was caused by an eclipse. Other researchers have pointed out that only a lunar eclipse can occur on Passover, when Jesus was crucified, and lunar eclipses can't be seen at midday. That's one disinterested party who appears to have confirmed a key fact in the Bible."

"Interesting. And, I'm impressed with your ability to recall facts, but that's a trivial detail," Ben said, amazed that as tired as Dan must be, his passion and knowledge seemed readily at hand. To be honest, Ben was enjoying the intelligent discussion, even if he didn't buy it.

Dan stopped for a few moments to think. Then he said, "All right, a Roman emperor named Julian, who lived around AD 360, wrote a lengthy multivolume tirade denouncing Christians. Historians and Christian apologists who have answered Julian's attacks point out that Julian actually provided proof of Christ's supernatural powers."

"Such as?"

"Let's see. Julian excoriated Christ for not doing anything miraculous other than healing the crippled and the blind and driving demons out of people. He even mentioned that Christ walked on the Sea of Galilee and calmed its waters, but he tried to negate the event by claiming it could be explained by natural events. In his attack, Julian actually confirmed Christ had performed miracles."

"That's all well and good, but ancient writings about a human being who could perform magic tricks are not conclusive historical evidence supporting the existence of God."

"Actually, you're wrong. The Bible makes it clear that Christ was God in human form."

"And what might that historical evidence be?" Ben asked.

"A lot of people who are a lot smarter than me have studied the subject and concluded that not only did Jesus Christ exist on earth, but he was executed and then reappeared in physical human form. More than five hundred eyewitnesses saw Christ in the flesh after his death. No other self-proclaimed messiah has ever done that. His actions, not just his words, demonstrated he was the Deity."

"That's nothing but hearsay."

"It's eyewitness testimony, and when Christ's apostles wrote about the miracle of Christ's resurrection, many of the people who physically witnessed Christ alive after his crucifixion were still living at the time. If the apostles had lied, they would have been denounced and their writings would have been totally discredited. Instead, no one contradicted them, and their testimony stands to this day."

"You're tenacious, I'll give you that. Your so-called proof is interesting, but you haven't convinced me."

Dan shrugged. "What's just as compelling is that every significant event in Christ's life was foretold by the ancient Jewish Scriptures—the Old Testament."

"I don't believe that."

"It's a matter of record."

"Where?" Ben asked. "Where is this indisputable record?"

"Ben, you're a Jew. Didn't you study the Jewish Scriptures when you went to synagogue?"

Ben's face colored. "Some, when I was a boy—a long time ago, Dan. A lot of Jews don't read the Scriptures today," he replied.

"I didn't know that. The Jewish Scriptures make up the Old Testament in the modern Bible. They contain prophecies that are crystal clear in their predictions."

Dan rummaged through his backpack and pulled out a spiral notebook with scores of makeshift tabs made from yellow stickies. He scanned the handwritten notations and opened to a page.

"Here's a good example, Isaiah 7:14: *Therefore, the Lord himself will give you a sign: the Virgin will be with child and will give birth to a son and will call him Immanuel.* That's an exact description of the birth of Christ about seven hundred years before it took place."

With his finger tracing the handwritten passage, Dan read out loud: "Take Psalm 22, verse 1: *My God, my God, why have you forsaken me?* That's exactly what witnesses heard Christ say on the cross hundreds of years later."

Ben retorted," Rabbis never talked about anything even remotely connected to the New Testament—it was forbidden."

"And here's verse 14: *I am poured out like water, and all of my bones are out of joint*; verse 15: *My strength has dried up like a potsherd, and my tongue sticks to the roof of my mouth*; verse 16: *Dogs have surrounded me; a band of evil men has encircled me, they have pierced my hands and my feet.*"

Dan closed his notebook. "That's a description of the crucifixion written centuries before it happened. What's amazing is that the Romans hadn't even invented crucifixion yet; they didn't develop it until hundreds of years after the Old

Testament was written. There's a lot more I could read to you. I don't believe in coincidences. That description isn't just remotely close—it's right on."

Ben was surprised, but more upsetting was how angry he felt. "Look, they didn't really have us read the Scriptures. We covered a lot of meaningless material in prayer books. Besides, those so-called prophecies took place thousands of years ago. You can't come up with anything that has happened recently."

"I sure can." Dan flipped through his notebook and stopped at another page. "Here, Isaiah 17:1: *See, Damascus will no longer be a city but will become a heap of ruins.* We've seen some major damage to Damascus since the civil war began in 2011 and ISIS joined the fight. Whole areas of the city are almost uninhabitable now because of the widespread damage to homes and businesses. The destruction has started. Still need convincing?"

Ben shrugged and turned his head to the side. "Nice try, but that's a stretch."

"I don't think so," Dan answered quietly. "The fighting rages on and, little by little, Syria is crumbling, including more and more districts of Damascus. I'd call it prophesy in progress."

Dan stared at Ben as though waiting for him to speak, but Ben was out of arguments.

Dan continued. "I think most Jews have never had the opportunity to see how Jewish the New Testament really is. Take the first pages of Matthew. They talk about Abraham, the father of the Jewish people. Jesus Christ was a Jew and so were his disciples. They didn't convert to another religion after Jesus' death and resurrection. They remained Jews, but preached the gospel about Jesus Christ."

Ben remained silent.

"There was no reason for Jews to abandon the doctrine of faith in the New Testament. Unfortunately, sometime during the fourth century the Jews were cast aside as followers of Jesus Christ. What a pity. The greatest man who ever lived was a Jew, and for the last 1,700 years Jews have been trying to dismiss him as a mere prophet!"

Ben murmured, "We learned at a very early age not to mention Christ—like he was some kind of religious degenerate. Rabbis spent a lot of time dancing around the subject, avoiding it, and making sure it never came up in conversation. A believer in Christ can't exist in the traditional Jewish culture."

"A real shame," Dan stated as he looked squarely at Ben. "You know, the Bible is more Jewish than any other book you could read. Jews wrote two-thirds of it! It's sad that generations of Jews have been left in the dark about their direct ties to Jesus Christ."

"I'll grant you those passages could be considered compelling," Ben commented, "but you don't hear any discussion about it these days."

"You're right! The sad truth is the prophecies are covered by pastors and priests in the pulpit, but they're rarely presented outside of the church as evidence of the accuracy and relevance of the Bible. And you'll never hear any mention of it in any school, unless it happens to be faith-based and private."

As if he had been prodded by an electric shock, Ben straightened in his seat. Looking directly at Dan, he stated in a deadpan voice, "I'm still waiting to hear your so-called historical or archeological evidence."

"You're a hard sell," Dan said with a laugh. "I couldn't begin to rattle off all the historical evidence that has documented the life and actions of not only Jesus Christ, but many of the figures in the Bible. However, there is one piece of physical evidence that graphically documents that Christ was crucified, buried, and resurrected as described in the Bible."

"And what might that be?"

"The Shroud of Turin. It's a linen burial cloth many believe was found in Christ's empty tomb. The Bible documents that Christ was wrapped in a clean linen cloth after he was taken down from the cross and placed in the tomb of Joseph of Arimathea."

Ben snickered. "I know the story. That thing was discredited years ago. Didn't they carbon-date it and find out it was a few hundred years old? It's a fake."

"The carbon dating showed it to be about seven hundred years old, but there have been several developments since the dating that call that figure into question. First, the area where they removed the cloth sample may have been contaminated by a type of coating from microorganisms that would throw off the dating. Second, and I think, more importantly, part of the section that was dated may have been added as a repair to the cloth sometime during the sixteenth century, through a process called invisible reweaving. A forensic exam of the cloth showed the area that was carbon-dated was different from the rest of the shroud and contained madder root dye and gum on the fibers. Some researchers believe the material was added after portions were cut off and sold. Personally, what I find compelling is a prayer book from Budapest produced in 1192; it shows an illustration with a clear representation of the shroud, burn marks and all, that are in the precise location of where they exist on the actual shroud."

"I'm still not convinced," Ben said, though he wasn't as unconvinced as he'd once been. Is Dan really on to something?

"Okay. I think what's even more convincing is that modern scientific techniques have revealed the image of the person on the shroud is in photo-negative 3D form. Unlike any other image examined on a piece of cloth. The image shows the faint outline of a man who had been scourged severely, had wounds on his wrists and feet, a wound on his side, and bleeding puncture wounds on his head—where the crown of thorns would have been. Experts have tested and proven that the shroud has human blood on it, but no one can explain how the image was projected onto the shroud material. Tests have ruled out it's a painting or any other man-made image. Some honest scientists speculate that some form of energy transferred the image from the person under the shroud to the shroud material, but no one knows for sure."

Ben remained still and listened.

"There's another piece of companion evidence you don't hear much about—the Sudarium of Oviedo—a facecloth that was wrapped around Jesus' head at the same time he was wrapped in the shroud. Both have the same blood type on them—AB. A lot of the bloodstains on the facecloth match exactly the stain patterns on the shroud."

"Never heard of it."

"I'm not surprised. I think they're compelling pieces of corroborative physical evidence that confirm the manner of

Christ's death and the unique aspects of his time in the tomb, and his physical resurrection. Modern science can't duplicate the shroud."

"All circumstantial at best, to borrow your phrase. I still don't see why you place such significance in a couple pieces of cloth."

"Because the shroud shows an uncanny resemblance of the crucified Christ. Sort of a supernatural photo of his body that God's left us. It's an actual illustration of the defining moment of the Scriptures, and one thing more, too ...."

"You know, you've mastered the art of the pregnant pause. But go ahead, I'll take the bait. What else is it?"

"A receipt."

"What are you talking about?"

"The supernatural image of the crucified Christ, whose body was never found, was the perfect way for God to say that the soul of every man and woman who would believe in him was bought and paid for by Christ's sacrificial death. The transactional nature of Christ's death in our place for our sins is referenced throughout the Bible. God gave us a receipt to show that the transaction has been completed."

"You still haven't proven anything." Now Ben sounded indignant.

"Then, how about the Jewish Pharisees? The last thing they wanted was for the so-called myth of Jesus' divine nature to be perpetuated by the mysterious disappearance of his body. They wanted a rotting corpse that would prove they hadn't executed the Son of God. Now another shadow was placed over their hasty illegal trial and execution."

"Someone could have taken the body and disposed of it. Jerusalem had a lot of caves and wells in the area."

Dan shook his head. Ben started to speak, but was cut short by the sound of a chime. Both pairs of eyes shifted in the direction of Dan's belt-mounted phone.

"Sounds like a signal for me to go have a smoke," Ben said. "Go ahead and check your messages while I take a break."

# CHAPTER SEVEN

## *The Earth Is Flat*

"Richie, please, can we stop driving around? I'm not kidding you; I'm really in a lot of pain. I need to eat, I need some water, and we need to stop this and work something out. If not for me, then for the baby, okay?"

While the violent shaking had subsided some, his eyes burned from tears and fatigue. *What am I doing? A baby?*

He drove on in silence, glancing her way as he tried to think out his next move. He had to reach his father before the airport reopened. There was no other way. But maybe there was time to make her understand.

"Okay, the diner is probably still open. We'll circle back and go there, all right? You've got enough money in your purse for something to eat, and we'll talk. But Joy, you gotta promise not to make a run for it, okay? You do that, and I'm dead—and maybe you, too."

She nodded, obviously fighting back tears. "I would never run from you, Richie. I love you. I know you've got this sickness going on, but I know you can get better. I know we can make this work out."

He turned the truck around on the slick road and drove back the eight miles to the diner. A half-dozen cars sat in the parking lot, including a highway patrol cruiser. He was idling there. Richie could see flashing lights way up the road. Probably another ice-related accident.

He steered to the far side of the lot so he could watch the state trooper. In a few minutes the trooper left, and Richie sighed with relief. He pulled out his pocketknife and motioned for Joy to put out her hands. He sliced off the tie, and she rubbed her wrists hard.

"So," Richie said, "you think there's a way out of this mess? You have no idea what kind of people are after me for their money. They'll kill us all in a heartbeat. And God help me, I need more—and soon."

Joy reached out a trembling hand and touched his haggard face. "You don't need dope, Richie. You need hope."

***

A sharp rapping on the patrol car's window jolted the officer who was staring at an accident report in his idling cruiser. Startled for a second, Officer Paul Westin looked up and recognized the officer who was tapping with his flashlight. The power window strained under the heavy coating of ice as it whirred downward.

"I have an ID for your crispy critter."

He passed an evidence bag smeared with foam residue into the patrol car. Officer Westin shined a light into the bag and squinted as he attempted to read the name and number on the partially melted Virginia driver's license—only a few letters and numbers were legible.

"I'm gonna need more than this. I don't even have a readable plate. I'm going to have to do some digging to find out who this guy was."

"Whoever it was sure caused a mess tonight. Half of Charlotte's lost power because of him. Not the diner, though. Plenty of coffee and food still there." The officer shook his head as he surveyed the smoking remnants of the substation. He handed Paul a cup of coffee through the open window, the steam escaping out the tiny hole in the lid.

"Still can't believe he made it all the way through to the substation without hittin' a tree." He again paused as if the cold had numbed his senses. "Guess you've got your work cut out for you."

"Yeah, it never fails," Officer Westin quipped as he frowned and shook his head. "I always end up with the big ones. I'll be workin' on this report for a week," he complained. He took a sip of coffee while staring at the scene of fire trucks, utility vehicles, and patrol cars surrounding the substation. Most of the fire had been contained by the foam, but a few small pockets still sent flames dancing into the icy night air. "Thanks for the java."

"You're welcome. If this weather doesn't break soon, neither of us will make it home until tomorrow night. The wrecks keep piling up all over town," moaned the officer.

"I won't be leaving here for a while. I'm just getting started," Officer Westin responded in a resigned tone.

"Keep the faith, brother." The officer headed to his vehicle, his steps crunching the crystal-like coating of ice.

Officer Westin observed his fellow officer. A seven-year veteran of the force, Paul Westin had volunteered to keep the case when his watch commander had arrived on scene to take charge of the crash site.

Paul had once been a member of the Major Crash Investigations Unit (MCIU) and possessed the necessary skills and experience to lead the investigation of such a major vehicle accident. As he caught sight of the smeared evidence bag on the cruiser's passenger seat, he began to wonder about the accident victim.

Speaking aloud to himself, he started to recreate in his mind the horrific moments before the driver met his death. "You never stood a chance, bud. Now all we need to do is find out who you are."

In the distance, the lights from the Charlotte Douglas Airport complex were faintly visible against the ebony sky smudged with dark gray storm clouds.

\*\*\*

Lounging in what had become his temporary bed in the departure area, Dan pulled up the new text message on his phone.

"Welcome back—somebody has a tooth."

Dan knew immediately it was from his daughter Sarah, who was working the night shift at the hospital. She was a registered nurse, like her mom.

He tapped on an attached photo that filled the screen. A grinning baby with drool running down the side of his mouth brought a smile to Dan's face. Aaron was about eight months old now and starting to cut teeth.

Dan missed holding his grandson, and couldn't wait to pick him up again and take him on a tour of the house—his infamous art tour. Dan would describe every acquisition proudly to anyone who'd listen. He loved to hold Aaron up to a painting and watch him study the color and texture. There was something about a bond between a grandfather and a grandson that he couldn't put into words.

Just then, Dan caught the unmistakable limp of Ben out of the corner of his eye. He was surprised to see him back so soon.

"I didn't see a soul outside," Ben announced as he flopped down beside Dan. "Not a single car came past the terminal the whole time I was having a smoke. Hell, I didn't even see any salt trucks or plows—too dangerous to be on the road. Everything's coated in ice."

"So that pretty well seals our fate for tonight. I was still hoping they'd get us a late flight out after the ice storm stopped."

"Fat chance," Ben quipped as a gust of wind slammed frozen rain into the terminal windows near them. The windows were completely crusted with ice.

"I've never seen anything like this," Dan commented as he frowned and stared at the opaque windows. "I bet you there are a lot of trees down around here; that must have caused the power to go out. If they can't keep the heat on in here, we're in big trouble. This place will be like a morgue."

Ben nodded. His chest heaved up and down as he struggled to catch his breath.

"Aren't you getting tired of going through security to have a smoke?" Dan asked.

Ben leaned toward Dan's ear, and in a mock whisper, said, "There are only a couple of security guys down there and they wave me through. I look harmless."

"That's a stretch. I wonder if your daughter would agree with you. By the way, she must be disappointed you're gonna be a day late."

Ben fidgeted with his blazer and looked away briefly. "She doesn't know I'm coming."

"What? Are you kidding me?"

"No, I didn't want to give her the chance to tell me not to come."

"What if she's not home or she's busy? You're gonna show up unannounced on her doorstep?"

"Yeah. I've never been good at apologies—I could never do it on the phone. I might change my mind. If I'm standing in front of her, I'll do the right thing."

"I sure hope it goes the way you planned. I could never do that." Dan paused and collected his thoughts." I have to admit I haven't been the greatest parent myself. I've been blessed with great kids and we've been able to get along, in spite of all my faults. I was barely there as a father for my kids sometimes, but somehow they turned out fine, no thanks to me. I have to give my wife the credit."

After he finished his sentence, Dan realized he was bragging. He looked at Ben, whose expression stayed the same.

"You strike me as someone who'd be a pretty decent father," Ben said.

"I'm good at putting up a front. I was too detached when they were growing up. Not that I didn't care about them. I was too wrapped up in my job—the result of a fear of failure, and being a borderline workaholic. That ultimately led to my career becoming my religion. I'd come home every night totally spent, and on top of that, I traveled a lot. It's a hazard of the business. The wife of a good friend of mine used to say her husband gave everyone at work his great side and when he got home at night all she got was the grump. I think a lot of us in our business were that way. You flip a switch in the morning and become pumped up to handle anything, and when you walk out at night, you flip another switch and the air goes out. You're an emotionless shell of a person at the end of the day. It's the stress."

"But you stayed married and have a relationship with your kids."

"My wife and kids learned how to compensate for my shortcomings. The truth is my kids grew up well-rounded because they saw the areas where I was limited as a person and made sure they didn't develop the same flaws. I know my parents were a huge motivation for me not to turn out the way they did. Don't get me wrong. They tried their best, but they were detached—especially my father. They never broke away from their own personal demons. I guess it was the Great Depression and World War II that affected my dad the most. They seemed stuck in life, trying to cling to what they had rather than thinking of ways to go out in the world and find more. Right now I'm trying to make up for my past by being a better husband and father. I also want to help others and not focus merely on myself."

"I guess that means your mission of saving souls."

"Yeah, I guess you could say that, but so far my track record is zero."

"Don't sell yourself short. I don't personally subscribe to your belief system, but you make some pretty decent arguments."

"Appreciate that. When I was an agent, I always liked giving briefs and trying to convince people of the truth, especially when they dealt with threats to people. Now that you mention it, I think I'm actually getting through to you."

"Nice try," Ben said with a laugh. "Remember, you're dealing with an academic. I live in a world where words and ideas are the only products we produce, and more and more these days, quantity is confused for quality. In your case, you're going to need both to sway me to your world view. So far, you haven't found a silver bullet, but I assume you have more, or is that it?"

"Oh, I have more. In fact, I have an interest that's more related to your world—a field of study that has some real potential for building a case for the existence of God."

"And what might that be?" Ben still had a trace of cynicism in his voice, but his defensive body language betrayed his faux arrogance.

"Near-death experiences. Are you familiar with NDE studies?"

"I'm aware of them, but I don't take them seriously, and neither do most of my colleagues. It's pseudoscience—another fringe element that claims to be an academic field."

"It may not be a traditional academic field, but it's a field of study that spans medicine, psychology, and religion. A number of your colleagues have done legitimate scientific studies of the subject. Now it's not a matter of 'Do they really happen,' but 'What's really happening and what do they mean?' Researchers have come up with some common terms and evaluation criteria that take it out of the pseudoscience realm, and they've compiled a lot of data on the subject over the past thirty or forty years."

"That may be true, but it's subjective hearsay. Why in the world would you put so much faith in a subject that carries the same academic weight as fortune-telling and astrology?"

"They're eyewitness accounts of the afterlife, provided by actual people who can be vetted. No sermons, no preaching— just people from all walks of life who have reported what they've experienced."

"What does that have to do with religion? I could understand a scientist's interest in a possible medical phenomenon, but what's the connection with your so-called faith?"

"What closed the loop for me was what some witnesses were reporting. Some claimed to have had experiences that could only be explained by drawing on what's written in the Bible. You've probably heard of the movie about a little boy who nearly died and claimed to have visited heaven and met Jesus."

"I vaguely recall some mention of the film, but I had no interest in seeing it. The imagination is a powerful tool— particularly if you're talking about someone under extreme stress."

"Many of the reported experiences can't be dismissed as the result of the mind creating hallucinations under stress. Many are very similar—not what you'd get if they were random dreams or mental malfunctions. You could easily dismiss the stories if only a few people came forward, but we're talking at least hundreds of thousands who all claim to have left their bodies and returned."

Ben arched his eyebrows and said, "Hundreds of thousands?"

"Many thousands have reported NDEs, but some estimates place the actual number in the millions—about 4 to 5 percent of the population. We don't hear about most of them."

"Why not?"

"You've confirmed they're not discussed in most college classrooms. I think a more basic explanation is that people don't feel comfortable sharing them. I suspect some people are still afraid they'll be ridiculed or considered crazy, but that's starting to subside now, with the topic entering the mainstream of our culture. Some of the more exceptional experiences have been documented in magazine articles, books, TV shows, and now movies. You have to keep your eye out for them, though. The reporting on them is hit or miss."

"If so many people have these episodes, where do their reports go?"

"I suspect it depends on who they tell. If they tell their physician or another medical professional, they'll probably go nowhere—although that's starting to change. Same if they tell a family member. They probably won't get reported if the person tells the clergy. The primary avenues people now have are foundations and other organizations devoted to the study of near-death experiences. Some of the organizations have established reporting mechanisms, like online questionnaires or blogs. It's strictly voluntary reporting and it's anonymous. That's where I first started to read about near-death experiences—NDEs—on websites. Then I bought books about folks who claimed to have had exceptional NDEs—like trips to heaven—so I could learn more."

"I'm still a little hazy on how a claim by someone who purports to have left their body is the silver bullet of evidence to support the claim that God exists."

"Because it's eyewitness testimony of people who have passed into a supernatural realm. It can be evaluated and tested. The scientific studies into the origin of life and the historical research about the life of Christ are very good, but I don't see anyone in our lifetime coming up with a smoking gun in either category. But now, thanks to modern medicine, we have live witnesses who have experienced their consciousness leaving their bodies and transitioning to a new destination in a different time and space continuum. In a small percentage of cases, people report having personal encounters with Christ."

"And why should anyone believe them? Anybody can have a dream or make up stories."

"You can make that case for any witness of any event. The key is whether their story is corroborated in every way possible. In some cases it's been done very well in NDE investigations. People need to take the information seriously."

"So the reports and studies meet your burden of proof?"

"In the cases that have been investigated extensively, yes. Now, there have been reported cases of fraud. One book in particular, about a boy whose parents claimed he went to heaven, was later withdrawn by the publisher after the boy recanted his story. So you have to be careful, but overall, I believe many are truthful and accurate accounts."

"All right, even if we do take the reports seriously, what does it mean?"

"It means the earth isn't flat! Most of what we think we know about the human brain and consciousness goes out the window. So does evolution, psychology, and psychiatry, to name a few. If our senses, thoughts, and memory reside in a location other than our brains, then we know very little about the true nature of man and the universe."

Ben shifted his position and leaned forward with his clasped hands resting between his knees. He said, "You believe there are enough credible people out there who have actually gone through a near-death experience that actually proves we have a soul? That there is an afterlife? That God is waiting with open arms?"

"Yes, at least a couple hundred people a day experience NDEs in the United States alone. There's a pretty consistent pattern in their reporting, and that's what got my attention. First, many people go through a separation phase, where their consciousness detaches from their body and lingers in the immediate vicinity. Many also report seeing their body while they float above it, and quite a few report hearing conversations of medical personnel and witnessing them performing medical procedures. Many report being drawn into some sort of tunnel or vortex and speeding toward a source of light during a transition phase; a substantial number report experiencing a life review—sometimes in the presence of beings of light. Some say they see dead relatives, and some are very specific about traveling to a location and seeing Jesus, or visiting heaven. A small percentage report visiting an empty void or a hellish place, and some report experiencing actual physical pain while being attacked by demonic creatures."

Ben shot his eyebrows up and down again, but did not speak.

Dan said, "Of the vast majority of positive near-death experiences, witnesses reported an enveloping sense of love, calmness, and joy. I have some issues with the percentage of positive versus negative experiences, but for now let's focus on the bigger picture."

"Don't you suspect these people are experiencing sensations caused by a dying body? If your brain is deprived of oxygen, it can do all sorts of things."

"Your brain essentially shuts down after about thirty seconds of no oxygen and starts to die in about four minutes," Dan countered.

"We still don't fully understand how the brain functions, so we can't say for sure it's not all a mental phenomenon," argued Ben. "Your senses still operate even if you're unconscious."

"That may be true, but what got my attention were the documented cases of where the patient was heavily sedated and then clinically dead for a number of minutes, and yet they reported observing specific activities in the operating room. In some cases, the person had audio suppression and eye coverings that would have prevented some of their senses from functioning, even if they were conscious. No hallucination could account for someone's ability to report back activities that actually took place while the person was sedated and unconscious or clinically dead with no brain activity. It's happened far too many times to dismiss the accounts as flukes or simply unexplainable brain activity."

"I've never read any of the studies, but I suspect they're not worth my time."

"That's my point. It should be a topic of conversation in the classroom and an area of widespread scientific research, not dismissed out of hand like you've done. Remember the report about CBS reporter Bob Woodruff?"

"No."

"He was wounded by a roadside bomb while serving as a correspondent in Iraq. He reported on national television about floating above his body after he was critically injured and knocked unconscious by the explosion. He reported seeing a white light. And what happened with the information? Nothing! Why isn't the scientific community jumping all over this?"

"Easy," Ben said. "It's anecdotal information. Not quantitative data. If NDEs were as important as you claim, then we'd all be studying them."

"It's critically important. It's the start of a new era in science and medicine! I think the reason many dismiss them is because of their implications for the academic and scientific communities."

"Let me guess. If they're real, a lot of careers would go down the drain," Ben interjected in a fatalistic tone.

"Exactly, but you know it shouldn't have to be that way."

Ben almost snarled. "You can't admit that decades of research were based on faulty premises and inaccurate facts. Most academics couldn't recover from a wholesale admission that they were wrong about the fundamental nature of man's mind and consciousness."

"Maybe some, if they continued to refuse to consider new findings and information. If the scientific community were to publicly support the concept that near-death experiences are actual events and our consciousness exists in an unknown form of space and time, it would be a starting point for a whole lot of new research into the brain, biochemistry, and the interface process between the brain and our consciousness. If our consciousness exists in another dimension, then it raises a lot of questions that invite serious research. How was our consciousness created? What is it made of? How does it interface with our physical bodies, and where does it go when our physical bodies die? Can we detect any sort of energy transfer when a person dies and their consciousness transitions to the next spiritual dimension?"

"Most researchers would find possible explanations that fit within their existing theories."

"True, but it shouldn't have to be that way. I don't believe the scientific community should be criticized for its good-faith efforts in research, but I do think it should be called out for ignoring the growing body of evidence that we have a soul. Scientists should be fascinated by the prospect, but instead they seem intimidated."

"Dan, I can tell you from personal experience that academics live off their past. Your research is your credentials. You can't throw all that away and expect to survive among your peers. I assume that's what you mean by intimidation."

"That's part of it, but I think it is more about political correctness and the huge secular bias permeating almost every aspect of our society. Many people know that truly objective research would probably cast the Bible in a new light, since it's the only written description of our soul consistent with the information reported by NDE witnesses."

Ben asked, "What's true objectivity?"

"Calling it like you see it and reporting honestly, even when the facts make you uncomfortable on a personal level. Most importantly, don't selectively pick facts that support your personal world view. Lay everything on the table and don't take sides."

"So, I suppose you thought you were objective in your line of work."

"Most of us tried to be, in my day. We weren't perfect, but the vast majority of us tried to get all the facts in every case, good, bad, or indifferent."

"Dan, do you mean it didn't matter to you if you didn't solve your case or get your man?"

"Sure it mattered—but not above all else. We cared about getting the facts and reporting them truthfully. I'll give you an example. Years ago we developed a suspect in an espionage case that had gone unresolved for several years. We had strong evidence that one of our foreign enemies had recruited someone working in our military to spy. The spy could have been a civilian employee or an active duty officer or enlisted. We had no idea of the age, gender, or any details about the potential subject. We had what we called an unknown subject, or UNSUB case. We knew the specifics about when and where the subject had met with his hostile handler, so through a couple of years of narrowing down a large pool of suspects, our analysts came up with a marine corps officer who we believed was in the immediate vicinity of the location where we knew a meeting between an American spy and a foreign intelligence officer had taken place."

"I don't suppose this ever made it into the news."

"It didn't. It's still in the classified archives with a lot of other unsolved cases."

"Doesn't that bother you?"

"Yes," Dan replied, "but it can be solved sometime in the future, and I'm satisfied we gave it our best shot. We prepared for months for confronting the suspect during an interrogation. We created special graphics to use during the interrogation, as visual aids to lay out our case, and we had a team of agents standing by to conduct a polygraph exam and a thorough search of his home."

Energized, Dan stood up and said, "Now all of this was taking place right after the first Iraq War started—Desert Storm—and the suspect was preparing to deploy to Iraq to be a spotter—someone who went behind enemy lines to give out target coordinates for precision munitions strikes. It was his last weekend home with his family—perhaps forever."

Dan stepped closer to Ben's seat. "I'll never forget when he arrived at our office for the interrogation. He was an impressive-looking marine corps officer—fit and well-groomed—he could have been on a recruiting poster. His expression was emotionless, but I could detect some tension when he came into the interrogation room and sat down. He was clearly shocked when we told him he was suspected of espionage, but he retained his composure and waived the military's equivalent of his Miranda rights. He didn't hesitate to agree to talk, and that was the first indication we might not have our man."

Dan saw Ben was content to sit back and listen, so he continued. "I started the interrogation by walking him through the events of the day in question. He readily admitted he was actually in the vicinity of where the foreign intelligence officer had been spotted. We got him, I thought! It was a remote area in a foreign country where few American military personnel would venture, and there could be no other explanation for him being in that location—or so I thought. I watched him carefully, monitoring him for signs of deception, but I saw just the opposite reaction. He told his story without missing a beat and never deviated once when we rephrased the questions in different ways, looking for discrepancies."

"Why was he in the area?" Ben asked.

"To visit an orphanage! He missed his wife and kids while he was deployed and wanted to be around less fortunate kids, to cheer them up. We checked out his story and, lo and behold, there was an orphanage near that location."

Dan sat down again and said, "My partner and I each had more than ten years of experience doing interrogations at the time, and we suspected he was telling the truth. We had to go through the process, though. The interrogation room had been set up with audio and video coverage—other agents were watching and listening to the interrogation from another room. We took a detailed sworn statement that locked him into his complete denial, and then we introduced him to our polygraph examiner who was standing by."

"He agreed to take a lie detector test?"

"Yep, and he sailed through the test with no problems— no deception indicated. Then we moved his poor wife and kids out of their house and into a motel—all with his permission, of course, and we proceeded to do a painstaking search of their home, reading his personal papers, looking into every nook and cranny—all in an attempt to find tradecraft—pieces of spy equipment a foreign intelligence officer would provide to his recruited asset. After combing the house for hours looking for concealment devices, communications gear, and hidden panels in his walls, we came up empty."

"Sounds like you blew the case!"

"Just the opposite. Now I was real disappointed we hadn't found our spy, but I was very pleased with the way the interrogation, PG, and search had gone. Why? We had exonerated an innocent man, a man who comported himself with honor and dignity. If I had had the authority, I'd have given him a medal on the spot for his conduct. He and his poor wife and kids never complained when we essentially ruined their last weekend together. We did our job. We hadn't found the spy, but we had cleared an innocent man. That's how the system should work. Let the chips fall where they may, and never get personally invested in the outcome."

"So you really think these NDEs, or separation events, as you call them, are that important?"

"I do, Ben. If you believe in God, then the existence of so many NDEs is confirmation that God allows individuals to return to their physical bodies by choice, and he does not erase their memories—at least not in all cases. I also believe some NDE witnesses are manipulated by evil spiritual entities. But by and large, though, most individuals are able to come back and report their experiences as accurately as they can. God is obviously not trying to hide the existence of the afterlife; he wants people to know about it! Some of the more compelling NDE witnesses confirm that they were sent back to tell their stories. It reinforces what's written in the Bible."

"You've made a huge stretch. Even if you can prove your consciousness exists in another dimension, it's not evidence to support the existence of God, and I don't see the connection with a book that's nothing more than a collection of popular tales."

"Over time, I think scientists will recognize that the Bible is a science book as well as a history book. The Bible even documents what Apostle Paul described as a possible out-of-body experience, or OBE. The Bible is the only reference book addressing both the existence of the physical and the spiritual worlds here on earth."

"You didn't explain how NDEs prove the existence of God."

"Even if you reject the existence of God, it's not scientific to dismiss out of hand, reports from many thousands of eyewitnesses who all report similar experiences. If you corroborate some of the accounts of the hundreds or even thousands of people who have had encounters with Jesus Christ, then you begin to build a credible case for the existence of God."

Ben said, "If the numbers are as large as you say they are, you could be right, but I rather doubt it. Good luck in getting the scientific community on board, though. I can tell you there are a whole lot more scientists who are atheists than believers."

"Scientists who study NDEs don't have to be Christians, they just have to be honest and have an open mind. Let the facts lead them to whatever the truth is. Don't be driven by an agenda. We did the same thing all the time in our cases."

Ben once again became silent. Dan could sense he was pondering thoughts that were disquieting to him. Allowing him to mull their conversation over in his mind, Dan kept quiet and wondered what would happen next.

# CHAPTER EIGHT

## *Wired*

"I knew you'd be up. I need a favor." Paul Westin scanned the laptop mounted in his cruiser as he talked into his cell phone to his brother-in-law, Gil Chandler.

"You're workin' nights again? Who'd you piss off? This is the worst night of the year to be out on the road," teased Gil.

"Tell me about it. I swapped with a guy months ago so I could take off and hunt, and now it's payback. Are you on your computer?"

"You already know the answer. Nothin' else to do now that Susie's gone. Besides, I can do some work from home and stay caught up. I hate gettin' behind."

Paul could hear his brother-in-law typing on his keyboard, and smiled a tired smile.

"Must be something hot for you to be callin' me this late," Gil said.

"You can say that again. I've got a John Doe from a real bad truck crash at the substation by the airport. Must have had 50,000 volts surge through that rig after it hit—damn near melted part of the frame. Worst vehicle fire I've ever seen.

Body's burned beyond recognition; it's gonna take a long time to get a positive ID. Can't get a readable VIN number from the rig, either. That's why I'm calling."

"What's the rush? You've never been excited about a traffic fatality before. Why's this one special?"

"I don't know. There's something about this one I can't explain. I feel the need to ID this guy as soon as possible."

"So what do you want from me? Sounds like you need a medical examiner and a metallurgist. I don't do accident scenes."

"Remember when you showed me how you could log in to all of the DOT security cameras around town and get real-time street views? I need you to see if you can get the video for tonight for any of the cameras on hotel row. This truck had to have come off of 85 and headed south. Somehow he got onto Keeter Drive. I need a still frame with a readable plate number of every tanker truck that took the Little Rock Road exit between 1600 and 1800."

"That's gonna cost ya."

Paul laughed. "It always does. I've got some tickets to the race. You buy the beer."

"You got a deal. Let me see what I can do."

Paul disconnected the call, confident that Gil would have success. He took a deep breath, began craving some caffeine, and thought about the man who was like a brother to him.

They'd gone through the law enforcement academy together and had become close friends. After graduation, Paul continued on as a patrolman, but Gil excelled at anything related to computers and transferred to the Cyber Crimes Unit of the Charlotte-Mecklenburg Police Department's Criminal

Investigations Bureau. There he earned the title of "digital wizard." Any complex crime that involved computers ended up assigned to Gil. He eventually married Paul's younger sister, Susan, who died last year after a short battle with aggressive ovarian cancer.

*Been a long, hard year for Gil. For all of us.*

Westin eased his cruiser over the thick coating of ice, onto the main road in the general direction of the Charlotte Douglas Airport. And maybe he'd check out the diner for a restroom break and some coffee and something hot to eat.

\*\*\*

Inside the increasingly chilly terminal, the vibration of Dan's cell phone jolted him out of a restless sleep. He looked over at Ben, who was sitting partially upright and snoring loudly. His head drooped like a slumbering beast, slowly rising and falling with each labored breath.

Dan moved quickly out of earshot to take the call.

"Hon, were you awake?"

He thought Connie's voice sounded surprisingly energetic, considering the late hour. "Uh, I must have dozed off, but that's okay. Jet lag's catching up with me." Dan squinted at his watch—1:15 a.m. "Everything okay?"

"Yeah, everything's fine," she said. "I've been watching the news. There are wrecks all over the East Coast and a lot of roads are closed. I know you want to get home, but please stay there until this is over. Some poor man was fried in his truck a few hours ago. Lost control on the ice, they figure. Wasn't too far from the airport there, from what they said."

"Wow, that's horrible. But you don't have to worry. We're trapped here by the ice." Dan paused for a second as his mind cleared. "What are you doing up? I thought you were going to sleep after I called earlier."

"I did. But Sienna called. She's having contractions."

"Oh, damn. I feel like a heel. I promised to be there for her big day!" Dan had planned his trip home to be with his youngest daughter who was expecting her first baby. "Has she gone to the hospital yet?"

"I told her to call the doctor and stay put until the pains are about five minutes apart. She's worried about what to do, and Phil's getting nervous. He wanted to take her to the hospital right away."

"You know I want to be there, but it's impossible right now—what they're saying on the news is right. The roads around the airport are closed and the power's been going off and on all night. I think the ice took down a lot of trees and power lines. We've gotta be on emergency generators. I don't see how we'll get out of here by seven in the morning. Please tell Sienna I'll be there as soon as I can, and call me if anything changes."

"Okay. I'll call when we leave for the hospital. Dan?"

"Yes?"

"Have you seen Stan again? Had a chance to think on that any?"

He smiled. She'd always been his guiding light. "No, I haven't been wandering around, but I might get up and stretch some, now. I'm still thinking about what you said. Keep us all in your prayers. I've got you all in mine."

"You've got a deal. Love you," she said, and then she was gone.

Pangs of guilt rushed over him. He had to get home in time, somehow. Sienna was the family's miracle baby. She had been born three months premature when Dan and Connie were stationed overseas, and her early arrival nearly killed both her and Connie. Dan still vividly recalled the ordeal of Sienna being flown to a US military hospital while a doctor used a hand respirator to keep her alive. Dan had vowed he'd be there when she gave birth to her first baby. *But maybe God has other plans for us all?*

He looked over at Ben, who was still snoozing in the seat. Unable to sleep, Dan donned his backpack and Ben's briefcase and strode through the silent concourse, thinking of home. He knew Connie would keep Sienna as calm as possible, but he also knew Sienna would remember Dan's promise.

As Dan had grown older, he'd become closer with his daughters. Each of his girls was different, and they were all beautiful in their own way. He felt extremely blessed to have them and he realized the best gift he could ever give them was his presence during important life events.

Wary of another encounter with Stan Crofton, Dan took a different route, away from where he'd seen him last. *What is he doing here? What would I say to him, anyway?*

As his pace quickened, he felt a chill settling in the air. He realized the heat had stopped working and wondered how all the families with small children would fare.

He rounded the corner and strode into a concourse that branched to the left and then separated into left and right departure wings. He chose the concourse to the left, which had a cavernous departure area for international flights. It was packed with sleeping travelers scattered on the terminal floor.

Dan noticed one family by themselves on some deserted rows of seats.

As he got closer, he recognized the young sailor and his family from the food court. The father had his arms wrapped around his young sleeping son, who was dressed in a short-sleeved shirt and lightweight pants—not nearly enough clothing for the sudden cold temperature. One row over, the mother slept soundly on her side, with her infant daughter cradled in her arms.

As Dan walked near, the sailor opened his eyes and looked in Dan's direction. Dan held a finger to his lips.

Dan slipped his jacket off and started to hand it to the sailor. "He's gonna need this," Dan commented in a soft whisper.

The sailor shook his head in protest, but Dan draped it over the sleeping boy. The sailor gently sat up and quietly acknowledged that he and his wife had mistakenly packed their children's jackets in their checked luggage. Dan assured him it was a spare.

Speaking in hushed tones to avoid waking the small boy, Dan said, "I can't count the number of times we left something behind or under-packed when we did a transfer. You're going to need all the help you can get. Is this your first trip overseas?"

"Yes, sir, for both me and my wife. We were trying to get to North Carolina where my wife is from, but they gave us Naples, Italy. A lot of people want to go there, but I wanted to stay here in the States."

Dan sensed frustration and apprehension in the sailor's voice. He earlier sensed the wife's discomfort with their circumstances; now he understood.

"I think you'll really like it once you get settled in. Europe is a great place to live, and Italy is beautiful once you get used to the crazy traffic and the hot-blooded Italians. They're great people, though, and they'll love your kids. Italians love children."

"I hope so."

"What do you do in the navy?"

"I'm a corpsman. I had a chance to get into the navy's medical school program, but my wife didn't want me to be a doctor. She didn't want me to be on call all the time and have to work long hours. I specialized in EMT and trauma care instead. I'll be assigned at the navy hospital in Naples."

"If you look at the assignment as an adventure where you'll see and learn new things, you'll be able to adjust and enjoy it. If you can, let your kids learn Italian while they're there—they'll thank you for it later. Same for you and your wife. Learn as much as you can about the history and culture, and your tour will be a lot better."

"Yes, sir, I guess you're right. I appreciate the advice."

He wished the sailor well and made his way back through the terminal. As he strolled in the direction of the gate, he caught Ben's unmistakable limp out of the corner of his eye.

"I thought you were finally getting some sleep," Dan said, approaching him.

"I did doze a while. I was looking for a TV monitor with some news about the tornado and then I went out and had a smoke," Ben replied. Winking, he whispered, "My new friends expedited me through security again."

"I took the liberty of bringing your briefcase with me so I could get up and stretch while you slept," Dan revealed as he handed it to Ben.

"No problem. There's nothing in that old thing anyone would want—except me. I've had it since I was an undergrad—it was a gift from my father."

"He must be proud of you being a professor."

The two walked casually through the deserted concourse as they talked. Dan deliberately adjusted his gait to Ben's plodding pace.

"He passed away before I graduated," Ben said. "Multiple strokes destroyed his mind and most of his body, and then he gave up. The poor bastard lived a hard life and then lost his health. I've definitely gotten his genes. I'm not in much better shape now, and I've had an easy life."

"So he never knew you became a professor."

"No. He spent his late teens and early twenties hiding from the Nazis in Europe. My grandparents helped him get on a cruise ship that sailed out of Germany, only to have it turned away here in America. The ship took him back to Germany, and he somehow got off and went into hiding. He lived on the run, picking up food and shelter anywhere he could, but he was never able to stay in one place for very long. He made it all the way through the war and was rescued by our army."

"Wow, what an amazing story! I bet he was a real fighter to make it through an ordeal like that."

"He was, but he never recovered from it. It took a lot of years off his life. He never talked about it, but you could see it in his eyes. He was physically present, but some days his mind was somewhere else."

"How about your mother?"

"They met in New York. After the war, my dad came to the States to live with relatives and my mother lived two doors down with her parents in the same apartment building. They met, eventually got married, and a few years later I came along. We moved from New York to Pennsylvania when I was five. My dad opened a clothing store in Philly; it was a trade he learned in New York. When I was young, Dad always told me he was going to pass the business on to me."

"Did he?"

"I couldn't see myself selling suits and ties all day, and after Dad got sick, he wasn't in a position to force me to do things anymore."

"What did he force you to do?"

"He made me go to Hebrew school when I was a kid, and I hated it. Most of my friends were Jewish and they hated Hebrew school too. I ended up going to a public school after my dad got sick and Mom had to handle more of the business. Even though we lived on a street with mostly Jewish families, I had a lot of non-Jewish friends in public school. I always identified myself as a Jew, though."

"I went to school with a lot of Jewish kids too," Dan said. "I never thought twice about it. We all got along."

"What about your parents?" Ben asked. "Are they alive?"

"Mom still is. Both my parents also had a rough time when they were growing up. My dad's mother died when he was young, and he got shipped off to relatives in the South during the Depression. Right after high school, he was drafted and got sent to Europe to fight in World War II. He flew about thirty-five bombing missions over Germany in a B-17. He never fully recovered from the stress of combat, but he did his best to provide for us.

"No such thing as post-traumatic stress syndrome in those days. You sucked it up and went on with life. And like your father, he was haunted by his past. He didn't handle stress well and he had a tough time relating to us kids. I wasn't much help either; I added to his stress by being a wise guy when I got older. I wish I knew then what I know now. I would have been a whole lot more supportive of my parents rather than always thinking about myself."

"Dan, you know that being self-centered is part of being young. We all went through it, though I suppose I never fully grew out of it. I see it every day in the classroom. It's hard to connect with this generation; they're the most self-absorbed group I've ever seen."

"Agree with you on that. Getting through to millennials can be a real challenge sometimes."

Ben nodded, and then took a swig from a soda. He spied a row of empty rocking chairs haphazardly lined up in the main atrium. As they talked, he steered Dan to a couple of chairs facing the ice-crusted glass enclosure for a much-needed breather.

After settling into the rockers, Ben said, "I'm convinced their brains have become part digital device. Kids today spend most of their lives staring at screens—even when they're walking around campus. Half the time they don't even look up to see where they're going. What's worse is they have to text constantly and take photos of everything, and then they post it online. Who cares what you had for lunch? I don't need to see what you bought at the mall last night, but these kids have to record everything—they've become outside observers of their own lives—and it's not healthy."

Ben ceased rocking and angled his torso toward Dan. "I don't know how anyone could ever convince these kids that a higher power exists—they're too wrapped up in the moment. If it's not on the screen in front of them, it doesn't exist."

Dan frowned as he thought while rocking in his chair. "In some ways," he replied, "I think this generation might have the easiest time relating to a lecture about God and the supernatural, if they're approached the right way."

"Is that right? I'd like to see you in front of one of my freshman undergrad classes. You wouldn't stand a chance with your Bible spiel." Ben resumed rocking.

"I'm no professor," Dan said, "and I know you'd do a far better job than me, but if I got a shot at one of your classes, I think I'd take the direct approach. Hit 'em where they live."

"Oh?"

"I'd say something to jolt them out of their digitally-induced trances and get their attention, like reminding them they'll all be dead in the next sixty years or so, and some a lot sooner. Then I'd ask if they were concerned at all about what happens to them when they die."

"I don't think that would faze them," said Ben, with his trademark smirk.

Dan laughed. "Maybe not, but I'd tell them we now have circumstantial evidence that how they think and act today will have a direct impact on what happens to them after they physically die. Even if they thought I was full of it, they might pay attention. Then I'd mention that atheists and agnostics point to the lack of any visible signs of God as proof that no

Supreme Being exists, and that death brings a complete end to our existence."

"If they were actually listening, they might agree with that statement."

"I think they would. I'd finish by saying that we followers of Christ are viewed as foolish for believing in a supernatural world that no one has ever seen. After all, if there really was a heaven and a hell, we'd have some conclusive proof about their existence after more than two thousand years—right?"

"I doubt if it would work on a bunch of bored freshmen, but you might get the attention of a few."

Ben started to rock his chair slightly faster, and Dan increased the speed of his rocking as well.

"Then I'd ask them if there might be at least a small chance that what I'm saying is true. I'd say something like this: 'You know today's skeptics point out that there are no physical signs of any kind to prove God's existence. They scoff that religion is built around an invisible realm that must be accepted on faith alone. But stop to think about your daily life.'

" 'You wake up in the morning and probably stand in front of a microwave with your breakfast inside, while invisible waves of energy heat your food or coffee. No one has ever seen a microwave with the naked eye, yet no one disputes its existence. You get ready; head out for class, and check for text messages or tweets that were delivered to your phone by invisible signals. Again, you've never seen a text message float through the air, but you don't question its existence. You might listen to your car radio if you commute to campus, or maybe your smartphone through earphones. Again, you've never seen radio waves, but you don't question for a second that they exist—because you were taught that they do. After class, you settle back into your dorm room or apartment and check your Twitter, emails, and your Facebook page. More invisible signals that travel through wires or airwaves—you've never seen a tweet, an email, or any other digital signal, yet you don't question their existence.' "

Ben rocked in silence.

Dan summed up his thoughts to emphasize the point: "Electromagnetic waves, microwaves, radio waves, and all sorts of energy waves affect our lives on a daily basis. We never question their existence even though we've never seen them. Yet when we're asked to consider another form of invisible energy—a supernatural form—we dismiss the idea as nonsense."

"For good reason, I might add," scoffed Ben.

"Why is that? Has anyone seen someone's consciousness and been able to describe it? What does a memory look like in physical form? What does love look like?"

"They're not forms of energy," Ben shot out.

"What are they, then? They're not matter; no one has ever discovered a love particle. If you go through the Bible and interpret passages with today's scientific knowledge as a framework, you'll find multiple verses that seem to refer to invisible energy waves of different types that have always existed."

"Is that so?"

"Think about parts of Psalm 19, and I quote, *It rises at one end of the heavens and makes its circuit to the other; nothing is hidden from its heat.* Sounds like a description of solar energy to me. Men living at the time of Christ had no clue that invisible forms of energy existed, yet they believed instinctively that life was touched by invisible forces. Why did ancient man continuously seek out the presence of a God? You see references to why throughout the Bible. For example, Romans 8:16 tells us, *The Spirit himself testifies with our spirit that we are God's children.*

"When Christ inhabited a human body, he repeatedly showed his unique ability to alter the physical bodies of others through the use of supernatural energy he could tap into. When Christ confronted two men on the road to Emmaus after he had been crucified and resurrected, he blocked their minds' ability to recognize him, and then literally gave them a download of Scriptures into their consciousness. After he allowed them to recognize him and then disappeared, the men stated they had felt a burning sensation in their hearts while Christ was speaking to them. When a lot of energy gets transmitted rapidly from a source to another location, heat is usually a byproduct, and heat can burn a human body.

"We Christians have come to accept that the energy he accessed was the supernatural energy of God—the Holy Spirit. In some respects, it's no different than radiation. It can alter cells and change tissue.

"Ben, where does your conscience come from? Where do the pangs of regret or the waves of joy come from? I'll bet they're forms of energy we can't capture with today's technology—at least not yet."

Without expecting a reply, Dan said, "I'd then ask the class, 'Now consider why there are billions of Christians in the world today. Why didn't the written account of Christ's execution, resurrection, and ascent into heaven die a natural death, like so many other myths and fairy tales? You're all smart people. You don't believe in the Tooth Fairy or Santa

Claus, yet I know some of you here are Christians or at least have a belief in God. Why?'"

"People are like sheep and have a need to believe," Ben blurted out. He began to rock faster.

"Speak for yourself and your own generation. I think there's hope for some of the youngsters."

Ben rolled his eyes.

Not deterred, Dan said, "I'd then give a brief overview of NDEs and describe their relevance to the discussion. If I had the opportunity, I'd bring an NDE witness into the class and let that person tell their story. I bet some of the students would have a lot of questions and come away with a different perspective."

Ben said, "I wouldn't mind seeing that lecture myself, if you had an NDE witness. Have any of them gone into college classrooms?"

"I can only recall one instance, but suspect it's happened a few times over the years. The more famous NDE witnesses have made the rounds on the morning talk shows, and some speak at NDE symposiums and conferences. I think they'd make a great asset for teaching."

Ben snorted. "They'd be a novelty, but they still wouldn't solve your fundamental problem that the story of your Jesus is basically folklore."

"If the story of Jesus was just folklore," Dan said, "it'd be relegated to a couple of fantasy books collecting dust on library shelves in the fiction section. Why hasn't the story of Jesus Christ faded from popularity, like most stories? Why is the Bible the best-selling book of all time? I think it's because God sends us messages, subliminally, so we think about him even when we're not consciously focusing on him. We sense we have a creator who established the rules of the universe. We sense that how we live makes a difference. What's a conscience? The Bible suggests it's God's download of his principles that we know we should live by, as we instinctively know we have to breathe to survive."

"Download? Really!" Ben's eyes lit with amazement.

Dan nodded. "I can't think of a better way to explain it. And now, people should have a much greater capacity to grasp the principle, since we live with it every day. We're a download society. You know, some of the Scriptures describe the process that, when viewed through the prism of today's technological world, sounds like standard stuff." His right hand moved to grab something.

Ben said, "I know, you have a Bible verse—right?"

Dan grinned as he again flipped to a tabbed page in his notebook. Here it is. Hebrews 8:10. *I will put my laws in their minds and write them in their hearts.* Sounds like a download to me."

"It's a stretch, but I concede there is a similarity when you look at it in the context of today's wireless world."

"Hard to dismiss it out of hand, isn't it? God sends messages directly to our soul, like emails. I call them soul waves—sort of like sound waves, but different. The messages basically say 'Hey, don't forget me, I'm still here.' How's that for freshman Theology 101?"

"You've got quite an imagination, Dan. To be brutally frank, though, I don't think you'll hear any such message in classrooms anytime soon."

"You're right. What a pity," he said with a shake of his head. "I think God downloads different information to different people on an incredibly complex scale. Just as he was able to create human life, he can send billions of messages to people to influence them to make different but interrelated actions. He steers us in a certain direction, but he doesn't cross the line of impeding free will any more than pop-up ads in your computer compel you to buy something. You simply take it or leave it."

Ben slowed his rocking as he listened.

"If you look at our bodies with an open mind, and you take into consideration the growing body of evidence of the independent nature of our consciousness, or soul, you realize our physical beings are highly complex biological interface devices that send, receive, and process data which flows back and forth from the spiritual dimension." Dan paused in case Ben wanted to comment, which he did.

"You know; your ideas are sort of entertaining in a perverse sort of way. You've internalized your Jesus to an amazing degree."

"I don't see it that way. If you were to study the Bible at all—and I mean, including the New Testament—you'd see that the Bible, in parts, is a basic instruction manual for your body, which is a biomechanical device—an extremely sophisticated earth suit—that you are outfitted with at birth. No other book covers all the bases."

"So if what you're saying is true, and God is downloading information into your brain, as you say, why doesn't everyone jump on the bandwagon and become believers?"

"You have a choice to listen to it or ignore it. In today's world, it's easy to let all of the distractions drown it out.

Between Facebook, Twitter, videos, and TV, it's easy to drown out the quiet voice inside you. Some of those who actually sense the inner voice of God don't heed his call because of all the baggage that organized religions have brought forward from years of misinterpretation or misapplication of the Scriptures—and the criminal acts committed by some clergy. On top of that, look at some of the terrorism around the world today, inspired by a fundamentalist interpretation of Islam."

Jumping in, Ben said, "You finally made a point that makes sense. Organized religion has been the source of more man-made pain and suffering than almost any other cause in history. Why in the world do you still insist that a belief in God is a source of good?"

"We don't stop driving, knowing millions are maimed or slaughtered by careless or drunk drivers. We still buy cars every year. We don't reject medical doctors even though countless quacks and well-meaning incompetents have wreaked injury or death on unsuspecting patients. We recognize malpractice for what it is, but we continue to trust in most of our medical professionals, right?" Dan asked.

Ben nodded.

"The concept of God and the social constructions of organized religion are easy to dismiss if we're inclined to do so."

"It's all built on guilt and judgment!" Ben said in a raised voice. He rocked at a rapid pace. "No wonder religions are losing people by the millions. People have a hard enough life as it is, and then on Saturday or Sunday you want to bring people in and tell them they're no-good sinners who will roast in hell if they don't act like a Goody-Two-shoes!"

Dan smiled. "You make another good point. The message of God needs to be accurate but balanced. Most people have a hard time living life like God intended because we're always bombarded with suggestions that sin is good and just a natural by-product of living."

"Our culture is way past that," Ben said evenly. "I'm afraid you're fighting a losing battle. Kids today are awash in negative reinforcement. I think you're smart enough to recognize that much of our culture can lead you away from the Bible and down a completely different path."

"I know, but I think we can use parts of our culture to reach kids and introduce them to God in a more modern way. The key is to get kids interested and curious. That starts at home and in religious institutions, but it can be reinforced in school by presenting a balanced picture of the origins and makeup of mankind and the universe, including its supernatural aspects."

"Good luck with that," muttered Ben.

# CHAPTER NINE

## *The Three-Piece Suit*

Paul Westin let the dispatcher know he was going 10-7 for a badly needed break. After double-checking his cruiser, he headed for the door of the diner while scanning the half-dozen vehicles in the parking lot. *Weary travelers all*, he thought. Three salt trucks, a grimy red pickup ... and a dark SUV sat at one end, near the DINER sign. He recognized the white pickup of Derrick, the owner, and the black station wagon owned by the cook.

Someone had heavily salted the steps, which was a good move. Everything that didn't move fast enough was encased in ice. The police officer pulled open the heavy stainless-steel door and stepped into the warm alcove that housed the newspaper machines and two gumball dispensers.

He pulled open the interior door and stepped inside, taking a look around before going too far, a habit formed by years of police training. A young couple sat way down at the end farthest from the door, looking purely exhausted, by the stoop of their shoulders.

The road-salt drivers were at the counter eating breakfast, too tired to hold a discussion at the same time.

Paul nodded at the waitress—someone new. He turned toward the restrooms and took care of nature's call first.

Then he settled into the booth in the corner by the door. "What a mess this is, huh?" he asked the gum-chewing twenty-something who placed a menu in front of him.

She shrugged. "I'm getting paid to stay, so it works for me. Had more people in than I expected, and I don't have to try and drive home. I'm glad he stayed open."

"I am too, believe me. Just a cheeseburger, a large milk, and a large coffee to go, okay?" he said, handing her the menu.

"Sure thing. Be right back."

Paul reduced the volume on his radio until the nonstop stream of accident chatter subsided to the background. Then he checked his phone to be sure Gil hadn't tried to reach him.

Several minutes later, when the waitress brought out his meal, the young man in the booth down at the other end shouted a loud "No!" at the young woman with him.

She covered her face with her hands.

Paul could hear her softly crying. He sighed. *The impatience of youth. Do I need to go check on them, or are they just a couple overstressed from difficult travels?*

He took a bite of his burger and chewed, keeping an eye on that booth. The kid was signaling to the waitress, who sat behind the counter, setting up the large coffee urns to make more coffee.

Paul put down his burger and took it all in.

"Miss, Miss, I need the check now," the man called.

"I'll be right there," she replied.

The young woman in the end booth got to her feet and moved toward Paul. He watched, and when she shuffled past him, she turned her face away. She'd been crying a lot, by the look of her eyes. She headed to the restrooms.

Paul got up and strode toward the booth. When he got next to the young man, he smiled. "Been a long night, hasn't it?"

The young man jumped slightly and quickly looked out the window before forcing himself to look at Paul.

*What's that all about?*

"You have no idea how long it's been," the young man mumbled.

"Everything okay? Where you headed?" Paul asked. He had to be sure the situation was okay before he walked away.

The young man shook his head. "No, things are not okay, but we'll work them out. Tired, that's all." He nodded in the direction the young woman had gone. "She's pregnant and upset and all."

Paul sighed. No wonder they looked nervous. Probably hadn't even told their parents yet. He nodded and moved aside to let the waitress deliver the check. He took it before the young man could.

Paul said, "Since you two are going to be new parents, let me handle this for you, okay? And if you don't have to get back on the road tonight, don't. In another couple of hours, it'll be a lot safer."

The young woman returned to the booth and gave him a weak smile. She'd washed her face and fixed her hair a little.

Paul nodded at her and smiled. "You okay, young lady?"

She nodded. "We'll be okay," she said softly.

Paul winked at her. "Good luck, you two."

***

Gil Chandler clicked the mouse on his cluttered desk and stared intently at the computer screen. *Hot dog!*

"What are you doin', man?"

His question drifted into the cool night air of his dimly lit den as he focused on a still-frame image. A pile of computer towers and assorted computer gear lined the walls of the small room. He jotted down a number and grabbed his phone.

***

Paul Westin had just gotten back into his cruiser and notified dispatch he was back on the road when his cell phone rang.

He recognized the incoming number. "That was fast," he said.

"Can you copy down some plate numbers?" Gil asked in his slight southern drawl.

"I'm pulling over right now. Give me a minute." When he had parked in the closed truck stop, he said, "Go ahead."

"Your tanker truck tag—piece of cake—only one tanker rig came off 85, onto Little Rock Road all evening, and I got two decent frames. It's a Virginia plate. I got all the numbers and letters but one. I can crunch some different combos and get the last one. May take some time, though, but I should get it tonight." Gil recited the partial plate number to Paul.

"Great, man. I owe you."

"Don't worry, I'll collect." Gil paused for a second. "Guess what else I saw?"

"What?" Paul knew Gil had a knack for coming up with something big anytime he helped on a case.

"I was trying to figure out why the tanker got onto Keeter Drive after taking the Little Rock Road exit. There aren't any gas stations on that road, so it didn't make sense. I called a buddy, who got me into the security camera systems for a couple of the hotels in the area, and I started going through that video and the DOT backups to find out why the tanker made a detour. A wreck on Little Rock Road made him change course, and once he got on Keeter Drive, a pickup truck cut him off and sent him into the substation. Take this down." Gil read another partial plate number.

"But this is the killer part," Gil said. "About an hour before your rig came into view, a female walked through the parking lot of the Courtyard Hotel. A male walked up behind her and stuck something in her back—looked like a gun, but it could have been a short knife. He pulled her into the same pickup and took off. Now, I don't have any idea why they'd be circling the area like that, but I got a clear shot of the tag as it was leaving the hotel parking lot. Only problem is, there was some mud or maybe salt on part of the plate, so I only have the first four numbers—but it looks like a Maryland tag.

"Truck was older, single cab, 4x4, I'm sure of it. It's dark-colored, I think. Couldn't get a good view of either the victim or the subject, but both look like they're young adults and under six feet. Victim might be young. Think she's a Caucasian in her early twenties—not certain, though. There was a lot of pixilation in some of the frames. Did dispatch put anything out on it?"

"Nope, not a word. Don't think anyone called it in," Paul replied. *Two young adults? What are the odds?* "Everyone's been focused on the storm and all the wrecks."

"I'm not surprised. I'll call it in for you. Stay tuned," Gil instructed him.

"I will. I'm gonna take a shot and see if I get lucky with the pickup. I saw one a little while ago. Let me know if you get anything else."

Paul carefully pulled his cruiser back onto the super-slick road and headed slowly in the direction of the hotel to look for the pickup. The couple he'd talked to in the diner had left before he did and the truck was gone when he had gotten back into his cruiser.

"Damn," he muttered. The roads were almost completely deserted because of the ice. He circled back around until he was called to another accident scene near the airport.

\*\*\*

Ben's multiple maladies kept him from falling into a deep sleep. He looked over at Dan, whose head rested against the wall while he lightly snored.

*Of all the seats I could choose, why did I pick to sit with this man? Or did I pick it at all? He's smart, he'd done his homework. Why is it so important for me to discredit him? And why am I so uncomfortable doing it? Not like me at all....*

"I must admit, you're doing a decent job of researching your subject matter," Ben stated in Dan's general direction. He'd dropped any pretense of being the intellectual superior.

Dan stirred from his fitful slumber, with eyes closed.

"If I was younger, I might be more inclined to consider your concept of faith," Ben said, essentially talking to himself. "But I'm too set in my ways. I can live with myself the way I am. Besides, I've been in academia too long—the higher you go up the academic ladder, the less you're exposed to people who challenge your views."

Dan stretched his neck and turned his bleary gaze to Ben.

"Once you get to a certain comfort level as a nonbeliever," Ben said, "you have no incentive to change. You fit in with the crowd that lives for today. I don't take well to arbitrary rules that don't fit my lifestyle."

Ben could see the fatigue in Dan's face. Still, he hoped they could continue their discussion. For some reason, it was important.

After a moment, Dan shook the sleep from his head and smiled. "I don't live by rules; I've developed a strong inner compass. I feel comfortable taking some actions and uncomfortable taking others. It's not something I necessarily think about; it's become second nature."

"But you Christians are obsessed with rules and commandments, and to be frank, so are some of my fellow Jews." Ben began to raise his voice. "Your Bible is filled with thou shall not do this and thou shall not do that. I can't live a tightly controlled existence where all of the pleasure is weighed and measured. Your whole life is rationed by your belief system."

"Not really," Dan answered. "Your Jewish Scriptures are the part of the Bible filled with most of the rules. The New Testament does away with strict compliance as the requirement for salvation, and replaces it with a doctrine of faith and grace. God knew man could never follow all the rules when he handed them down to Moses, so he allowed them to make sacrifices to atone for their sins. Sort of a conditioning for what was to come. God changed all of that when he sent Jesus Christ to earth to die in our place for our sins. The new requirement was for man to truly believe in Christ, and God would forget about all of his past sins. God governs the universe by laws, but he redeems the souls of men by a covenant of grace—his salvation by grace."

Ben thought about it. *Is that how this man doesn't judge me about my infidelity, my divorce, the cruel treatment of my daughter?*

Dan interrupted Ben's thoughts. "See what you're missing when you don't read the New Testament? You don't learn how to get your slate wiped clean!"

"Nice try, but I'll take my chances." Ben paused and then measured his words. "I suppose it wouldn't hurt to peruse your New Testament—strictly from a historical perspective. I've never heard anyone talk about this so-called 'get out of jail free' card you mentioned. What other nuggets of knowledge have I been deprived of?" Ben wished he could quit the sarcasm, but something about Dan's words frightened him. And he hated being frightened.

Before Dan could reply, the entire concourse went dark. The whir of the ventilation system ceased and all were in complete darkness. Murmur rose from the various waiting areas.

"Can you believe this? The ice must have taken down some power lines," Dan stated as he looked out into the darkened gate area. "I thought facilities this big were supposed to have their own generators."

Ben gasped. Anything but the dark! He battled to get a gulp of air and stop his body from shaking. He clasped his hands in his lap and kept his eyes tightly closed. *It will pass ...* as his thoughts trailed off, the main lights came back on.

"Ben, are you okay?" Dan whispered.

He shook his head, eyes still closed tight. "It's the dark. I can't take it."

"You mean you physically react to it?"

"Unfortunately, yes."

Ben opened his eyes, then wiped his face with a wrinkled white handkerchief. Looking straight ahead, he could barely get the words out. "I have a slight affliction. As you've no doubt noticed. It's called achluophobia. The Greek word is *scotophobia*—fear of the dark. Started when I was child and I never grew out of it. Don't know how or why I developed it, but I can't sleep at night without the lights on and I can't stay in any dark room. I almost never go to the movies."

"Didn't know adults had such a thing. Can you get treated for it?"

Ben sighed. "I could never admit to a doctor that I have a phobia. It's not the sort of thing I would ever discuss with anyone. You're the only one I've ever told, other than my wife and daughter. There are some things you learn to live with."

Dan looked at him for a long moment, and Ben hoped they didn't have to talk about his weaknesses anymore—at least not right now. Dan nodded as though he understood.

"Well, back to your question," Dan said. "I guess one of the subject areas I've been reading about that has interested me is the spiritual makeup of man, and I mean in a sort of structural sense. You don't often hear it mentioned in most churches, but the Bible clearly describes how man is composed of three components. I think it's an important concept directly related to the whole idea that God speaks to man through a sort of supernatural wireless system."

"Really?" replied Ben with a laugh. He wasn't sure what he'd expected to come out of Dan's mouth, but that wasn't it.

"Yeah, actually, according to the Scriptures, we're made up of our physical body; the soul; and the spirit, which is our supernatural body and connection point to God. Some say we're just a soul and spirit entity that inhabits a body on a temporary basis."

"Spirit? As in evil spirits?"

"Spirit as in *Holy* Spirit. I think our soul is a complex form of intelligent energy that can move from a physical body to a spiritual body—it contains all of our thoughts, emotions, conscience, and memory; it's us. While we're alive on earth, our brain is the organ that interfaces with the soul. Our soul is also the part of our being that is contaminated by sin at birth, and we add to the contamination by our sinful acts while we're alive."

Ben cocked his head to the side. "Okay. Earlier you talked about your so-called God downloading messages to humans. Where does his download go, into the spirit or the brain?"

"The spirit. For example, when a person goes through a true spiritual transformation and begins to have a true belief in God, the person's spirit is instantly cleansed and restored. Hence, the term *reborn*. God, through his use of the Holy Spirit, does his supernatural download: some of his Spirit into ours, and our spiritual component is changed.

"The download is kind of a basic Holy Spirit Package 1.0 that completely rebuilds the spirit and feeds into the soul like

128

new software. Our souls remain damaged from our sinful past, though, and we have to repair it the best we can—though it is never fully restored while we're in our bodies. I believe we can upgrade our soul through prayer, reading the Scriptures, and projecting love into our environment through actions. If we keep sinning, it stays at the basic 1.0 level and never develops into a more sophisticated and fully capable form."

"And you found *this* in what literature?"

"I pieced together the teachings I've heard from many different pastors and researchers. I'm paraphrasing it to describe the process I think takes place."

Ben grinned. "So that's how you believe our physical and supernatural bodily components coexist while we're alive?"

"Exactly. When our body dies, the spirit and soul detach and move around independently with all of our faculties intact—but they stay together in a discrete supernatural state."

"I'm still not real clear on the whole spirit and soul theory. So what's the spirit again?"

"That's a great question. If you take multiple passages in the Bible and combine the information with some of the descriptions that people who have transitioned to heaven or hell have given, it looks like the spirit is a separate entity—a form of super energy that also has some sort of mass in the supernatural realm. The Bible makes specific reference to the spirit and the soul being separate entities, even though one fits into the other."

Dan pulled out his notebook and began the now familiar skim through the pages. "Here it is, Hebrew 4:12: *For the word of God is living and active. Sharper than a double-edged sword, it penetrates even to dividing the soul and spirit.*"

"I can honestly say I have never heard anyone postulate what you've suggested," Ben said.

"I'm just scratching the surface, and regardless of who agrees or disagrees with my take, the Bible is packed with information waiting to be discovered. It's the only reference book we have that specifically mentions the spirit and the soul as separate entities."

Ben stared at Dan. *Is this guy a madman or a man of God?*

Dan went on. "A lot of NDEers talk about being 'one with the light' or 'one with God.' In a sense, that may be accurate since God's spiritual energy appears to bond with our spirit and soul when we transition into the heavenly realm. Once we're connected to God, so to speak, we can tap into his knowledge and love while still existing as an independent being. That's why I think NDEers say they know all of the answers in the universe when they're in heaven—because they're literally plugged into God."

"So you're saying God is a formless mass of energy and not a distinct being?"

"God continuously emanates a spiritual energy that is love. Only, I think it's highly intelligent and multidimensional. God's love has power, qualities, and capabilities beyond our ability to comprehend. We can't explain it, but many NDEers sense his powerful energy in heaven. And no, I think God does have a distinct form that emanates his enveloping energy of love. He is the Supreme Being of the universe. His essence is so powerful, though, I don't think you can clearly distinguish his distinct form because of the radiance of the energy he projects. If you could, I think we'd be surprised. The Bible tells us we're made in his image, so we must look like him."

"Have I got this straight? When you die, your soul and spirit turn into an angel or a demon?" Ben chuckled as he shook his head.

"You're still a person," Dan said in an even tone. "You become an immortal version of you, only more alive than you've ever been in this life. I think that's why the Scriptures repeatedly state that if you believe in Christ, you'll receive life. I think they mean life at a whole new level that we can't comprehend. I'm sure it's a lot more complex than my description, but I bet it's close. After our death, we look like our physical bodies—only better—at least in heaven."

"Only in heaven? What happens if your spirit and soul go to hell?"

"That question fascinated me. When I read some of the extended NDEs where people went to heaven and assumed a physical form, I noticed most of the witnesses reported receiving a spiritual body that was around thirty years old, while others were their true age at the time of their death. Some of their relatives were older, but they all looked great. They became a perfect version of the physical body they had here on earth. Some reported that although they were blind or crippled on earth, their reconstituted spiritual body could see or walk in heaven. Your senses are enhanced too—you have almost 360-degree vision and telepathy. So from what I've gleaned, you're perfect by human standards, and you don't age. You stay your perfect self for eternity. That's why they call it heaven!"

"Does that mean I won't be a smoker and can breathe like a normal human being?"

"You've got it. One more reason to believe," Dan shot back with a grin.

"You know, there's a sort of perverse logic to your wild theories. I can see why the feebleminded might be attracted to your world of fantasy."

"They're not my theories!" Dan said, throwing up his hands and letting them drop. "I'm merely piecing together what I've read and learned and confirmed, as compatible with the Scriptures."

"All right. At least you have an interesting take on the subject, and I have to admit, before tonight I knew nothing about NDEs or separation events, as you call them. I guess if I go to hell, I'll still have this damned emphysema. It'll probably be tough, with all the smoke and fire …."

"Whoa! Be careful what you wish for, Ben. From what I can tell, your description isn't far off. The relatively small numbers of comprehensive NDE accounts from witnesses who describe what happens when our soul and spirit congeal in hell describe a process that's not pretty."

Ben thought, *No, no, don't tell me!* Instead, he said, "I'm all ears."

"Witnesses have described several different types of distressful near-death experiences. Some seem to be frightened by the entire transition of the spirit and soul, while others report ending up in a black void. Others are mocked by either seen or unseen entities; many report feeling the sensation of falling or going through a tunnel, and they end up in some distinct location that contains anything from mind-numbing boredom to stark terror. For those who end up in hell, the same general process that takes place in heaven also happens—but with one catch."

"Yeeessss …."

"According to some NDE witnesses, if you were blind on earth, you'll still be blind in hell. Likewise, if you're crippled or handicapped in any other way, you'll keep your handicap. But that's not the worst part."

"Don't tell me. The devil picks you up with a pitchfork and barbecues you like a chicken breast."

Laughing, Dan took a deep breath. After a brief pause, he turned and looked Ben in the eye. "Whatever you did to others while you were alive, you get it back—over and over. The worst part is that your new body can experience pain and emotion just like the physical one you have now—plus you have the memory from your time here on earth, so you remember the pleasures you enjoyed and can no longer have."

"You don't fade into oblivion?" Ben wondered how anyone could live, anticipating such torment. *Worse than life on earth?*

"Not from what I've read. Based on what some of them report experiencing, fading into oblivion would be a whole lot better than hell. Regardless of what part of hell you end up in, you'll have new neighbors."

"Let me guess—"

"You know where I'm going with this: demons."

Ben let out a deep belly laugh and shook his head, smiling. Some people trying to sleep nearby grumbled. "You've seen too many movies," he whispered.

"That's the reality, as far as I know, and I bet the vast majority of folks who go to hell and return never tell anyone, or only a few family members or close friends. People who have gone to hell are usually deeply scared by the experience, and many don't understand what happened to them."

Ben shook with laughter again as he enjoyed the humor in Dan's description. He cut his laughter short, though. "What was that comment you made about having a problem with the number of positive NDEs versus the negative ones?"

"First, I think a neglected area of NDE research is its general lack of coverage of negative or distressing NDEs. Most websites allow their postings, but some devote almost no attention to them. A few have done some good research and written books to report their findings, but they are in the distinct minority. Some researchers have even said that negative NDEs were beyond the scope of their work."

"So how did you get all of your information about hellish NDEs if most researchers aren't tracking them?"

"Besides reading the few books on the subject, I've sifted through many hundreds of NDE accounts on the Web to find maybe several dozen or so that appeared to be credible and fit the pattern of a true NDE. By and large, the vast majority of books on NDEs focus on positive or blissful experiences."

"Why's that a problem?"

"Focusing only on positive NDEs distorts the reality of what people are truly experiencing during their brief transition to the afterlife. I've seen some declare that based on the overwhelmingly positive nature of NDEs, the afterlife is a wonderful experience that all enjoy—regardless of how they've lived their lives on earth. I think it's terribly misleading and, worst of all, it gives credence to the position of some that a good God would never send his creation to hell, and they cite all of the positive NDEs as their proof!"

"And you believe that's not true?"

"No. All the biblical evidence points to a just God. Why bother sending Christ to pay for our sins if they don't matter?"

"Sounds like you want people to go to hell."

"Just the opposite! But you can't convince people to take a threat seriously if the threat is hidden from view or dismissed as a fantasy. We need full and complete reporting on as many NDEs as possible—good and bad—so people truly know what they face. Also, reading the Bible once in a while wouldn't hurt."

"Has anyone ever told you you're paranoid?" Ben asked, wondering if paranoia might account for Dan's devotion to the topic.

"More than a few times. But I wear it as a badge of honor."

Ben laughed. "You would, I suppose. So what's this grand conspiratorial theory of yours?"

"You know there's a Bible passage that sums it up." Dan pulled out his notebook and started flipping through the pages.

Ben fought the urge to roll his eyes. They both needed sleep badly, but he knew if they stopped talking, he wouldn't sleep.

"Here it is." Dan traced a passage with his finger, and read: *For such men are false apostles, deceitful workmen, masquerading as apostles of Christ. And no wonder, for Satan himself masquerades as an angel of light. It is not surprising then, if his servants masquerade as servants of righteousness.* That's 2 Corinthians 11, 13 through 15," Dan announced as he shut his notebook.

"I think I know where you're going with this, but go ahead."

"I believe some of the beings of light that witnesses are experiencing during their NDEs are demons. Some masquerade as angelic beings or loved ones from the witnesses' lives on earth. And why would Satan and his demons want to give NDE witnesses false positives? So they come back and say, 'Gee, I was a sinner who didn't repent, but I got into heaven! We don't have to worry about how we live. We all end up in the same place anyway!'"

"You've got a sick mind ..."

"I've got a well-trained mind. Looks like a satanic deception operation to me. Now, I know a lot of folks would disagree with me, but I'd be willing to bet many of those short and sweet NDEs would have had a very unhappy ending in the long run if they'd continued and the witness hadn't been resuscitated. One of Satan's names is the Deceiver."

"You definitely have a unique way of interpreting facts, but what's all this have to do with your belief that we are a walking three-piece suit?"

"NDEs and OBEs are important because they are experiences of people who have left their physical bodies and traveled in their spirit bodies. The spirit is the supernatural connection point that God has with us while we're on earth. That connection point didn't always exist as it does today."

"I'm not following. Are you saying man didn't always have a spirit and a soul?" Ben asked.

"No. God created Adam and Eve with a spirit and a soul, but they had direct access to God, who was present in his spiritual form in the Garden of Eden. Prior to being physically and spiritually corrupted by sin, Adam and Eve were able to connect with their spirits and have direct access to God in his spiritual form. After they sinned and were evicted from the Garden, they lost their ability to directly access their spirits, and their access to God was degraded. God then began his work to reestablish a relationship with man in his fallen, sinful state. For a long time, he had to literally appear externally to man. God appeared as a burning bush to Moses, gave Moses the Ten Commandments on literal tablets of stone, and he appeared as a cloud or a flame to the Israelites after Moses came down from the mountain. God continued his pattern of appearing externally to man until one eternity-altering event."

"You've lost me completely."

"Through the life and death of Christ, God changed his method of direct communication with man. He no longer had to appear externally as a flame or a cloud with a booming voice. Once Christ died and completed God's master plan of reconciling a sinful human race with a sinless God, God flipped a cosmic switch and energized his new spiritual communication system."

"I take that back. You've lost *it* completely."

"Hear me out, Ben. Right before Christ was crucified, he told his disciples he would be sending them a counselor to take care of them once Christ was gone from earth. What he was really telling them was that God was going to change the way he communicated with those who believed. He would no longer need to enter our earthly realm in some sort of physical form—he would use the Holy Spirit to communicate with us, internally. And what is the connection point in each human? Our spirit! God would no longer need to be external to us since he was now going to connect with us internally, in a literal sense."

"So what? How in the world is any of this important? Who cares whether God appears as Casper the Friendly Ghost or becomes a bad dream? What difference does it make?"

"It makes all the difference! It explains how God can be on this earth and not be seen, yet he is felt. How many times have you seen some sort of disaster and then people say 'How could a good God let this happen? How could he let all of these people die? Where's God?' "

"Dan, for once, you've nailed it. If there was a God, we wouldn't have earthquakes, tornadoes, or terrorists. A true God would stop them!"

"Ah, but you've nailed it. Man commits acts of terror, murder, and mayhem, and natural disasters are part of life on a fallen world that became cursed after Adam and Eve sinned. But we *do see* God every time a person risks his or her life to save a person from a burning building or a raging flood. God acts through man, and in order for him to do that, he needs a connection point, and that point is our spirit. Every time we see an act of sacrificial love or selfless kindness, we see the power of God in action."

Ben didn't reply for a moment and then reengaged. "That's quite a spiel. How many others buy into your view of the universe?"

"My hypotheses come from the excellent research of others. Actually, you happen to be my captive audience today, and honestly, you're the first stranger I've opened up to with this. I've discussed this with a few select friends, but that's it. I really don't feel ready to defend my beliefs in prime time— yet." He looked around, then back at Ben. "That's why I'm doing the book. I know my ideas and observations are solid."

Ben sighed. His mind needed a break. "You sound pretty well prepared to me. You have a good mind for detail, and you can think and present opinions logically. I wish more of my students thought like you do. That's going to be some book when you get it written."

"Thanks, I'll take that as a compliment," said Dan as he tucked his notebook away and got to his feet. "Seems like your decision to visit your daughter is having some side benefits," he said with a weary smile.

Ben shook his head. "Don't get too cocky. I said you presented a good argument—I didn't say I'm buying it."

"You will—I'm not done yet."

Ben could hear the smile in Dan's voice as he walked away.

# CHAPTER TEN

## *Skunks at the Party*

"I'll make everything better. Give me time. Give us time!" He steered the pickup toward a sign that read AIRPORT DEPARTURES. The headlights caught the reflecting tape on a line of traffic cones blocking the road to the terminal.

"Don't try to go there—can't you see it's closed?" she cried. "It's still closed, Richie. I thought you were okay, I thought—"

He shook his head. "That cop was a little too nosy for me. I need to get to Dad and get that money. Once the airport opens and he flies outta here, he'll probably never speak to me again."

"That's not true. He loves you. I love you."

Ignoring her, he switched the truck into the 4x4 mode and mashed the gas, knocking over several of the orange cones as the pickup plowed forward on the deserted road.

They approached the departure area in front of the terminal. A uniformed security guard standing by the curb waved the truck away with his flashlight.

"Airport's closed! Can't stop here," the guard shouted through cupped hands.

"Damn it!" Richie pounded his fists on the steering wheel. He slowly accelerated and headed back into the airport exit lane.

\*\*\*

Ben took the last puff from his cigarette before grinding it into the receptacle as he watched the taillights of the pickup fade into the distance. While he ambled along his now familiar route back to the departure gate, the telltale flicker of lights caused him to quicken his pace.

Within seconds of Ben's flopping down next to Dan, the power went out again and all were greeted by immediate darkness. Within a minute, emergency lights came on, but their weak yellow glow barely illuminated the gate area, and the heating system was now off. Ben again winced and fought to control the urge to panic.

"I guess I'm finally going to get the therapy I need—the hard way," Ben announced.

"Wait," cried Dan. He fished through a small side pocket and pulled something out. "Here, this should help."

Ben took the small flashlight. "Thank God. You've had this all along?" He hated how frantic he sounded.

"Yeah, sorry. I forgot I had it," Dan said with an apologetic smile.

Ben clicked it on and started to relax. After a second or two, he realized what he had said. "I just thanked God, didn't I? I guess we all slip sometimes. Shows how deeply imbedded the concept of the Deity is in our culture."

"I think it's more basic than that. You're wired to believe, even if you fight to repress it."

"You might be right," Ben said. *Why does what he says feel so right? Am I getting soft in my old age, or is he on to something?*

"This storm is more than anyone can handle. It's gonna get real cold in a hurry in here if they don't get the power back on soon." Dan reached for his backpack and pulled out a spare light jacket.

Ben shifted in his seat to get comfortable and noticed the name "CHIEMSEE" printed over the right breast pocket of Dan's jacket. "Do you understand what you're wearing?" he asked sternly.

"This jacket? Oh, you mean, Chiemsee?"

"Yes. That was one of Hitler's early projects, you know. My father mentioned going to that lake as a child, before the Jews were rounded up and segregated from the population. I visited the area during one of my trips through Germany. Beautiful spot on the Autobahn."

"Yeah, I guess we wear things and don't realize the effect on others. I never gave it a thought. I bought this as a souvenir when I stayed at the Lake Hotel run by the US Army. I heard that Hitler had the Rasthaus complex built before the war. We used to go there for bilateral meetings with our European counterparts while I was assigned overseas. The Germans hosted CI conferences every year or so, and I represented NCIS there and in other parts of Europe."

"So, counterintelligence, or CI, as you put it, is a primary function for most governments, I take it?"

"It is. Great Britain has MI5. Their counterintelligence and domestic security agency, and some of our agencies are loosely patterned after their functional components. Countries have to defend themselves against spies and hostile intelligence services. No matter what country they're from, CI operators are pretty much the same the world over."

"Are they as dedicated to their work as you seem to be?"

"I would say so. Most are pretty persistent and naturally curious."

"I'd have to say you've brought that same passion to your work of studying the Bible."

"I don't consider studying about the kingdom of God to be work—it's more of a personal calling. I think the same can be said for my previous line of work. You feel called to work in law enforcement and counterintelligence."

"Sounds like an interesting career, but I suspect it has drawbacks," Ben said.

"Only a few. The biggest adjustment in CI is that you can't discuss your job with your family or friends; most of it's classified. Also, after you've been in the business a while, you lose interest in the artificial aspects of life. I don't like sitcoms anymore because they're contrived. Same for most shows that deal with espionage and counterintelligence—they're usually the product of someone's imagination who's never worked a day in the profession. I can't watch 'em."

"I've never been a fan of spy novels. I don't read fiction, but I do like an occasional spy movie. There's something perversely entertaining about watching devious adults double and triple cross each other. Am I using the right terms?"

Dan laughed. "You're close. There are assets, or agents, and double agents. There are recruitments, penetrations, and walk-ins—all terms of the trade. One of the biggest mistakes I see Hollywood and the press make frequently is their reference to CIA case officers as agents—there's a big difference. The word 'mole' is also used a lot by Hollywood and the press. It would take all night to explain what they all really mean. Did you happen see the movie, *Tinker Tailor Soldier Spy*, based on a John le Carré novel?"

"I actually did, on a flight a few years ago. What a bunch of scheming bastards—everyone screwing everyone over while keeping a straight face. I love the deadpan look of a true backstabber. You have to be at least mildly neurotic to do that job—don't you?"

"It doesn't hurt to be a little skeptical," Dan said. "But really, the most important quality is to be grounded in the present, focused on facts, and hungry for the truth."

"I thought you were always digging for overlooked clues that will tell you what happened in the past."

"True, we do look for clues and information about past acts, but the most effective CI is preventing the damage from happening in the first place."

"Sounds like you come from a distinct subculture with your own vernacular and code of conduct. How is a *spy catcher's* quest for proof that God exists different from anyone else's?"

Dan shrugged. "I think we bring a different mindset and some unique training and experience. But using the skills I developed over the years is the key. For a topic as complex as God, I took a multidisciplinary approach, like we did in the intelligence community. We'd take signals intelligence, imagery, human source reporting, and various physical measurements, and blend them together to get the big picture."

Ben nodded, though he was amazed at such a different way of life from his. Dan had done and seen things Ben couldn't even imagine.

"My line of work dealt primarily with human sources, but we also used products and services from the other disciplines. The field of study with the biggest potential for greater insight into the kingdom of God, in my opinion, is the near-death experience. The basic research that's needed starts with good, solid interviews or debriefings, like we'd do and then analyze in the intelligence community."

"Isn't that being done now?"

"Most of the accounts from NDE witnesses come from self-reporting on NDE websites. That's fine, but many of the witnesses would be able to provide much richer accounts if they were interviewed by a professional."

"I take it you believe folks with your background could help glean information that could prove God exists."

"No one can prove God exists in a concrete sense—at least not yet—but you can build a circumstantial case so convincing, it's hard to reach any other conclusion. I think using some of the same tools I used when I was working would go a long way in building a solid case in today's secular world."

"Wouldn't a scientist be better suited to track down evidence of the afterlife than a cop? Some of your folks seem pretty paranoid."

"I think our mindset and methods make us the ideal profession to look objectively at the issue of the existence of

God. Some have called us the most cynical SOBs to walk the face of the earth. We even had a Deputy Secretary of Defense call us the 'skunks at the party.' Why? We have the reputation for being the most distrustful and suspicious folks of any profession in existence today. We suspect everyone of being capable of doing wrong—no matter how high their rank or station in life. We've seen people fail and succumb—even our colleagues. Look at what happened to General Petraeus."

"He did lose control."

"We have to maintain control and think rationally to do our jobs—we filter out emotion and biases—we deal with reality and accept nothing at face value. I can't think of any profession that is potentially more antithetical to religion than counterintelligence. Religion is practiced by people and we don't trust people—period. People lie."

"You don't even trust each other?"

"People who've been vetted usually trust each other, but there are more than a few examples of bad apples. Look at the FBI's Robert Hanssen and the CIA's Aldrich Ames—both sold out America. And remember Jonathan Pollard?"

"Wasn't he Jewish?" Ben asked, searching his tired mind for the name and association.

"Yep, and he worked for NCIS as an analyst. When it comes to our profession, we trust, but verify—to use a hackneyed phrase—and that's why we undergo a new background investigation every five years and take polygraphs. It doesn't catch everyone, but it's an important step."

Ben looked at Dan for a long moment. "Okay, there's bad eggs in every profession. I haven't always been a paragon of virtue, as I've told you. Other than a corrupt insider, what's an example of a threat to our national security that most people don't know about, Dan?"

Dan shrugged. "Some specific budget cuts."

"That didn't take long," Ben said with a smile. He really liked this man.

"If the budget for our national security elements is cut deep enough and salaries don't keep pace, the quantity and quality of the people hired goes down, and potentially the integrity of some organizations will go down along with it. You have to have new blood coming up through the system on a continuous basis so that people with the right skill sets and experience are doing the job at all times. Draconian budget cuts prevent hiring and leave organizations with generational holes in the experience level of their workforce."

"Are you saying we'd have a bunch of crooks working at the FBI?"

"I've worked with the military, law enforcement, and national security agencies of more than twenty foreign countries, and I can tell you from experience that the lower the pay, the more the corruption in a country—without exception. You can't pay a colonel or a police chief $15,000 a year and expect him not to look for ways to supplement his income. Once someone takes dirty money, it's a slippery slope downward. Penetrating an agency in a country where everyone is underpaid is not hard. We're starting the descent. The government does very little efficiently, but one thing it must do is protect us from external and internal threats—and that takes decent salaries and pensions."

"I get the impression your line of work is underappreciated," Ben said.

"To an extent, you're right, but it's gotten much better. Everyone always understood the need for us to do criminal investigations, but a lot of commands felt uncomfortable about our counterintelligence mission; they didn't understand why it was necessary. When our primary focus was on foreign intelligence service threats—a very elusive threat—we weren't popular in the wardrooms and barracks. We used to go in and give briefs on how everyone was vulnerable to approaches from foreign intelligence officers, and folks looked at us like we had two heads.

"I remember giving a threat brief to a commanding officer of a naval fleet intelligence center in the early '80s. At the end of the brief, the CO, a senior navy captain, told me that all of his people were of the highest caliber and his real worry was the cleaning contractors who had access to his building."

Ben nodded. "Sounds reasonable."

"Yeah, but a few months later a couple of NCIS and FBI agents visited the captain and informed him that one of his petty officers had contacted the Soviets and offered to pass nuclear-strike war plans. That kind of ruined his day. A few years later, the poor captain committed suicide. I can't prove his suicide was the result of his sailor being a spy, but I'm sure it added to his grief."

"Ouch. I bet that made you popular."

"No one wants to admit that they or their people are vulnerable to a recruitment pitch or susceptible to going bad and volunteering to work for the other side. It's like admitting you're flawed. But once Hezbollah and al-Qaida ramped up their attacks and we built up our combating terrorism program, the navy and marines were much more receptive to us. Now they could relate to an identifiable terrorist threat. Suddenly we were very welcome at almost every level."

"You know, you've given me an idea of what the subculture of CI is like, but you haven't made your case for why you seem to think CI folks are well-suited to make the case for God."

"To start with, CI is in the people business, and God works through people, and so does Satan. Missiles don't launch themselves and wars don't get started by machines—at least not yet. People go bad—they commit evil acts. We focus on the motivations of people, and the driving forces that motivate people really come from their soul, in my opinion."

"Interesting concept. I've never heard it put that way."

"CI, positive intelligence, and most of the law enforcement world are the only elements dealing simultaneously with the body and the soul. We fingerprint people; we gather trace evidence from crime scenes—all for the purpose of dealing with the physical world."

Dan took a deep breath and shifted in his seat. "But we also delve into the soul without consciously thinking about it. We deal with actions that are prompted by anger, jealousy, and greed, all of which come from the soul and are governed to some extent by our conscience. You may argue that our conscience is developed through the socialization process, but I believe it's a key component of our soul. What's our conscience? Nobody knows, but we all know that virtually every sane person has one. It's our character, in a general sense—it's the internal compass that guides us—our right-and-wrong meter—or as you would probably say—our error correction instinct."

"I'm glad to see you're still on planet Earth."

"Only criminal investigations and national security operations—and CI in particular—zero in on the conscience as a tool. To be fair, the clandestine case officer world—the foreign intelligence collectors—also use some of the same tools. How do we do that? A number of ways. The polygraph, or lie detector, is one of our tools, but we also use a whole host of vetting methods that tap into the conscience. And that, my friend, is tapping into the soul."

"Lie detector? No one puts any faith in those things. They're not even admissible in court!"

Ben knew that much to be true after being married to a lawyer all those years.

"True. Lie detectors, polygraphs—PGs, as we call them— are just a tool, but one based on scientific principles. We're not talking hocus-pocus, Ouija board stuff. The modern PGs are very sensitive computerized instruments that measure galvanic skin response, respiration, and certain muscle contractions."

Ben laughed.

"If I hook you up to a PG and ask you if your name is Ben Chernick, you'll say yes without giving the answer a second thought. No physical reaction. But if I ask you if you've ever cheated on your income taxes, and let's say for the sake of argument that you have, you'll tense up a little even if you're willing to tell the truth—because you know it makes you look bad. The machine will pick it up."

"You've convinced me never to take a polygraph," Ben said with a snort.

Laughing, Dan continued. "Don't worry, your secrets are safe with me. But seriously, if I asked you a question that you didn't want to answer truthfully, you'd most likely have a physical response."

"Like I said, they're not admissible in court, and a lot of people beat those things, anyway."

"That's true. Some people get through them while lying, but actually, in most cases they beat the *examiner* and not the machine. The key is the explanation for the reaction. In some high-profile spy cases like Aldrich Ames, the subject, or examinee, had problems with the exam, but he was able to convince the examiner that his reaction was related to another issue. Now with computerized machines it's a lot more difficult. The bottom line is that any machine is only as good as its operator."

"Even if a person passes a polygraph, that doesn't mean, say for example, that they went to heaven. They could be insane and actually believe they went to heaven while they sat in their padded cell." *Okay, Mr. CIA man, think about that one!* Ben sat straighter in his seat. This old man can still debate!

"True. Just because someone passes a polygraph exam doesn't prove the person went to heaven or hell—it shows the person truly believes they did—and that's a major hurdle. The use of the polygraph in the case of NDEs would be valuable to flush out fabricators—and they can be a big problem. Some of the pushback you read about in book reviews of NDE witnesses is that their stories have no outside corroboration. Worse, the skeptics claim that NDE witnesses are out to mislead with contrived hogwash and a not-so-hidden agenda. If you can show the witness is truthfully reporting what they believe happened, then it disarms some of the critics. The basic but very powerful message of clearing a witness with a polygraph is that their message should be taken seriously."

"Did you run into fabricators in your work?"

"Yeah, and they were a big problem."

Ben was surprised. "Really? Did you see that many?"

"Not that many, but all it takes is one to tie your office up in knots for days or longer. I can think of one right off the bat and he was a major drain on resources. Even one can keep you from focusing on the real threats at a critical time."

"Give me an example of what a fabricator would do."

"I remember someone called an NCIS office overseas where I was working and claimed a terrorist group was planning to drive a truck bomb into the local American Consulate. The consulate was in a foreign port city near one of our regional field offices, and we had scores of agents ready to respond, while the CIA had its only officer assigned to the area on leave and the FBI was hours away at the main embassy. So we went to the chargé d'affaires and laid out what we had. The chargé, or chief of mission, told us to run with it. In those days we had an excellent relationship with the US country team and the major players—CIA, FBI, and Diplomatic Security. The chargé made sure everyone was notified, and we took the lead.

"The caller provided detailed information about the attacker and their methods—he knew the area and the methods of real terrorist groups that were active. Our first step was to vet the caller, but since the time frame for the alleged attack was to be within forty-eight hours, we also had to take steps to set up and detect acts by the alleged attackers. The caller claimed he did not trust the host country and would not work with them, and, as I recall, he had a convincing story as to why he didn't trust them. I remember he claimed he had a relative who was falsely accused by the host country for a crime, and therefore he wouldn't deal with them. That put us in the position of trying to work clandestinely to vet the caller without alerting the host country or the alleged terrorists.

"We spent the next two days doing around-the-clock surveillance of the area near the consulate, plus some pretty intricate steps to coax the caller to a meeting so we could surveil him and learn as much as we could. We set up a command post in an apartment that overlooked the area near the consulate. He kept feeding us information that made sense, but he began to try and manipulate us when we wanted to set up a meeting. For the safety of our special agents, we had to control the time and location of the meeting. Long story short—when we began to detect him being deceptive with us, we made the decision to bring in the host country. We set up a meeting that he finally made, and the host country confirmed he was a serial fabricator and the threat was a hoax."

Ben didn't get it. "Why would someone do something like that?"

"They have a perverse psychological need to feel important. In this case, the caller wanted to tweak the host country, too. They ended up arresting him for making a false report. It gets back to your conscience—but in this case the person had a severely impaired one or one contaminated by evil."

"So you think that's a window to the soul?"

"Absolutely. Our sense of right and wrong, while it may be partially a product of our culturalization, or as you would say, socialization, comes from our soul. You can't give someone a pill and make them honest or caring. You can drug them up so they can't think clearly and have fewer inhibitions, but you can't change the motivations of a sober person with a chemical."

"That's it? That's how CI allegedly deals directly with the soul?"

"There are other ways. For example, we tempt people and evaluate their reactions. Clandestine case officers do the same thing, as do the more complex undercover criminal operations, but I believe CI makes the most pervasive use of temptation as a vetting tool. At least that was the case when I was active. One of the main goals of CI is to protect, and you do that by weeding out people working for you who are deceptive and motivated to deceive and steal."

"So how, exactly, do you tempt people?"

"We put them in situations where we think their weaknesses will surface."

"Give me an example."

"If we were vetting a person to work for us in a counterespionage operation—similar to what a layperson would call an undercover role—we'd put a temptation in their path while they were under surveillance and see how they reacted—do they give in and then lie about it to us?"

"So, do you have special training programs to teach you how to assess people?" Ben asked.

"Yep. We have a number of different programs—asset validation is one. It's become both an art and a science."

"All of this is somehow linked to the soul?"

"I believe our ability to resist temptation resides in our soul. If scientists could manufacture an anti-cheating pill, they'd make a fortune. Imagine thousands of households where the wife is standing by the front door with a 'Cheat Begone' capsule for her husband as he prepares to leave on a long business trip. She holds his nose and forces him to swallow."

"My ex would have ground them up and put them in my food," Ben said with a rueful laugh.

"Sounds funny," Dan said, "but she'd be indirectly medicating your soul if she did it."

He stretched his legs and looked at his feet. "We examine people's motivation in other ways," Dan said. "Do they pay their bills on time—in other words, can they honor a commitment? Have they committed crimes like major theft or assault on their spouse? Again, it's a window into their character and their soul."

*I wonder what this guy knows about me after all these hours ....* Ben felt the urge for a cigarette, but he wasn't going to follow it. *I'm in charge of my life, not the cigarettes,* he reminded himself.

He thought a moment. "Do you miss it?" Ben asked.

"NCIS, you mean?"

Ben nodded. "Yes. You worked and trained for years, you obviously loved what you did and thought it was worthwhile. So I'm wondering if you miss it."

Dan thought for a long moment, sort of chewing on the inside of his bottom lip. "When I started, the pay was low and we got paid very little for overtime. You didn't do if for the money, though—you did it because you believed in what you were doing. You saved lives—and often, the people you protected never knew what you did. But that was okay. You didn't do the job for recognition. NCIS has people you can trust, people who are true to their profession—people with passion for what they do. I miss the people sometimes, but not necessarily the lifestyle."

"You're kind of a closet zealot—you keep it pretty well hidden. But it comes to the surface every now and then," Ben said, his left hand covering a yawn. He hoped that most of the people in charge of protecting the nation were men like Dan Lucas.

"When it comes to my old agency and my work," Dan said with a shrug, "I'm proud to tell our story. I've spent nearly thirty years unable to share most of my days in the field with my wife and family; the work was mostly classified. When I get a chance to talk about the unclassified generalities, it flows like a river."

Ben smiled. He looked at Dan and slid down in his seat to get comfortable as another wave of fatigue overcame him. "I picked the right seat to sit in tonight. I must say it's refreshing to talk with someone who has a totally different world view. You must keep your wife entertained."

"She humors me. Might surprise you to hear that Connie and I don't discuss my research into faith that much. She has a strong one of her own and she gives me my space. I couldn't ask for more."

Fighting to keep his eyes open, Dan leaned back and turned to face Ben. He was already snoring softly.

# CHAPTER ELEVEN

## *Up or Down?*

The vibration of Dan's cell phone again roused him from a shallow sleep. Glancing at the phone with one eye partially open, he saw CONNIE on the screen. Immediately he knew something was wrong. Careful not to wake Ben, he quietly got up and strode from the gate area and took the call.

"Hon, sorry to wake you. I know it's late," she said.

"That's all right," he said, shaking the sleep from his brain. "What's going on?" He noticed it was 3:15 a.m. "Everything okay?"

"Sienna was admitted to the hospital. She didn't tell me she had a urinary tract infection when she called to tell me about her contractions. I told her to get to the hospital right away. Good thing she did. The doctors are worried the infection could spread to the baby, so they're going to treat her with antibiotics and then induce labor sometime later today."

"Why didn't she tell you about the UTI?"

"I don't know. I guess she didn't think it was important. She should be okay, but we won't know for sure until the baby is delivered. We have to leave it in God's hands, Dan."

He nodded. "I know. That's so much easier said than done. Keep me posted, but get some rest yourself. I want to know how both of them are doing when you get an update."

"I will," Connie said softly. "I'm sorry I woke you. Try to get back to sleep." She paused a moment, saying "I love you" before disconnecting the call.

He pictured the baby being born with a serious infection that could cause blindness or other serious complications. He quickly shut down his runaway imagination. He was a pro at concocting worst-case scenarios—a hazard of his business— but it never helped things. He knew Connie and Sarah would stay with Sienna and make sure the right medical decisions were made, but he still worried. *So much for faith, eh?* Seems he had several things to work on before he had the whole "leave it to God" thing licked.

He thought, *Nothing I can do from here but pray.* He silently made a plea to God to protect and heal Sienna and the baby. How would he feel if God didn't give him what he wanted most? Did he deserve to have his prayers answered? Maybe he'd track down Stan Crofton and work on some real forgiveness, like Connie had mentioned.

He scanned the area and decided against looking for Stan. If God wanted him to meet Stan again before they left the airport, God would make it happen.

Dan walked back toward his seat, feeling dejected that he wouldn't be home in time for the baby's birth. His profession had gotten in the way of a family commitment again. He paced through the dimly lit departure area while attempting to calm himself.

*Damn.*

\*\*\*

Ben was wide awake and scribbling on a notepad when Dan strolled back to his seat.

"Did my phone call wake you?" Dan asked him.

"No, I never sleep long. I've got sleep apnea and always wake myself up when I run out of air—helps keep me alive. I guess the one time I don't wake up will be when I find out if your theories are right."

Dan laughed. "I hope you find faith long before then."

"Don't count on it, my good man. Besides, at the rate I'm going, my number could be up any day now. But don't let that stop you. I'm enjoying our little discussions about the meaning of life."

Ben paused. He *was* enjoying Dan's arguments. He wasn't sure he believed them all, but the budding author certainly had his interest sparked.

After clearing his throat, Ben said, "That doesn't mean you've convinced me with your arguments, but at least you presented your case with conviction. I still can't understand, though, how someone with your background got interested in a philosophy that's essentially based on pacifism. You carried a gun, didn't you? Probably killed people too, when you had to, I'll bet. You are, in most ways, a warrior."

Dan nodded. "I did. But you're wrong about Christianity. We're in a battle against evil every day—we just use different weapons. In my case, it was a natural progression. I was born with the instincts to fight against evil, and that's what got me into law enforcement. When you stop and think about it, the field of law enforcement is one of the most biblically-related professions there is—right behind the clergy."

"How so? Because you tap into the soul? You made that point quite eloquently," Ben said, though he was truly interested in Dan's answer.

"It's part of it, but it's more basic than that," Dan replied with a shrug. "When you consider what we do, you realize we enforce some of the Ten Commandments—the law from the *Old Testament*. Thou shalt not murder; thou shalt not steal; thou shalt not bear false witness against thy neighbor. We chase murderers, thieves, and swindlers. Our profession is a world of dealing with the consequences of other people's sins."

"I suppose that's true."

Dan charged ahead and Ben fought a smile.

"They're very similar—helping to stop evil things from happening to good people is one of the jobs of the clergy, like it is with us. I guess since I always dealt with evil in the physical world, I was drawn to its parallel in the spiritual world. In my old job I tried to save lives; now I feel called to save souls. I think a lot of baby boomers from my generation are like the way I used to be: essentially decent at heart, but lost from a spiritual standpoint and headed to a really bad place for eternity. If you warn people about some impending harm, some will take action to avoid it."

"So you're saying that believing is essentially error correction?"

"In a way, yes. It allows us to take a corrective course away from our natural tendency to sin, but you can't correct an error you don't know you've made. That's where the Bible comes in. It has the information that can motivate us to take corrective action. If you're warned about a hazard, you have a choice of whether to avoid it or not."

Ben thought a moment, before formulating his argument. "Error correction is human nature that's refined and reinforced through physical trials and socialization; you don't need threats of fire and brimstone to activate that instinct in man."

"Depends on the type of threat," said Dan. "The threat from the consequences of failing to have faith can't be seen with the naked eye. I think the key is you have a lifetime to correct the error of not having faith, but many become complacent and never get around to facing the realities of life, and tragically, their error has eternal consequences."

Ben smiled through his exhaustion. His chest was feeling tight again, but in total, he didn't feel as bad as he might have if he'd been sitting alone on this miserable night.

He said, "Maybe scare tactics will get some people's attention for the short term. I'm not so sure they'll have the lasting result you seem to think people need."

"Don't forget that God is ultimately the key part of the process. I can deliver the necessary information, but God has to validate it in a person's soul if they're receptive."

"Why do you think people like me are able to brush off your sales pitch so easily?"

"It doesn't take any effort to dismiss something that makes us uncomfortable—or demands we change how we're living our lives. Few know what the consequences are. Plus you get help from the evil entities that get pleasure out of seeing humans lose their souls. People don't realize that their choice of whether to believe or not is the biggest decision they'll make in their entire lives. You have a choice of where you spend eternity, but you have to make the decision on your own. God isn't into forcing us to comply. He's given us free will, so we get to choose."

"A choice? Are you saying people control where they go when they die? I thought religion taught that God is everywhere and controls everything."

"From what I understand, there are two main schools of thought about free will and salvation in Christian theology: the Calvinistic view that God is in control of everything, and the Armenian view that while God is the ultimate power in the universe and does work to steer mankind in his direction, man has free will and therefore has a choice of where he'll spend eternity. I wonder if the truth is actually a blend of both."

"How so?"

"The Calvinistic view—which is based on a long-held interpretation of the Scriptures—is that God elects certain people to be saved and spend eternity with him. God makes the election—or the selection—and man is not part of the equation. I may be oversimplifying it, but I think I'm in the ballpark."

"If your God operates that way, you'd better hope you're in the lottery, right?"

"Exactly. I think what is actually happening is God elects those who he finds have a willingness to believe in him. It's a supernatural process that humans will never understand. Somehow, God knows the soul of each person and determines their willingness to have faith. They may not even be conscious of their decision, but nevertheless it happens. So after God does a reading of us, he continues to call to us if we are truly willing to believe."

"Whoa. You're going into the deep end here. You're saying we have control over a component in our soul that we aren't aware of?"

"Yeah, I think so. To give you a very crude analogy, look at our autonomic nervous system—it controls our pulse and respiration. We don't consciously think about our breathing or heartbeat; it happens automatically. But if we want to, we can consciously override our breathing and stop it altogether until we lose consciousness, and we can engage in relaxation techniques and slow down our pulse. I think we have a component in our soul that controls our God receptors, if you will. God gives everyone the same control system, but our own nature controls how it operates—independent of God.

"So, Ben, back to my point. A lot of times, we aren't even aware we are willing, but God is. That's why followers of Christ are needed to go out and awaken the willingness in each of us who wants to believe. Some of us are reached late in life, but we are reached through the efforts of others. I think that may explain how God intervenes in our lives, yet allows us to have free will."

Ben shrugged. "I've never read the literature on Christian ideology, but I can see why there would be a major debate on such a fundamental issue. I think the concepts are way over the head of most people, though, so I don't know how you'd be able to put the process into secular terms."

"You're a grandfather, right?" Dan asked.

"Technically, I am. My daughter has a seven-month-old son—at least that's what her Facebook page says."

"Your spy, the graduate student—right?"

Ben swallowed his shame and momentarily looked away. "Yeah."

"Okay, when your grandson reaches the age of accountability—sometime in his early teens—he'll be in a position to decide whether he believes in Christ. If your grandson does make the decision via his soul, to be willing to accept Christ and live as a Christian, then God will pursue him; hence he'll be one of the elect. On the other hand, if your grandson makes a conscious decision to reject Christ, then God will eventually withdraw from the boy and he'll fall into the other place. I think most people can understand that."

"Are you saying people send themselves to hell?"

"Exactly—hell is complete independence—you're permanently removed from God's presence forever, by choice. And—"

Ben interrupted. "Technically speaking, if your God is in control of everything and everyone on a constant basis—even in a passive sense—then *he* sends people to hell."

"Not really. Some Bible scholars have made a strong case for the interpretation of the Scriptures showing that God is not in control of man on earth on a real-time basis; he delegated his sovereign authority over the earth to Adam and Eve—like a landlord does when he, or she, leases a property to a tenant. God continued to own the world, but he delegated his authority to control activities on earth to Adam and Eve. When they sinned, they forfeited their authority or control over the earth to Satan. God returned sovereign authority to man on earth through the death of Jesus Christ and the blood covenant God made with man at the time of Christ's sacrificial death. Satan and his evil followers still exist and have access to us, but we now have the authority to cast them out of our lives if we are born-again believers. It's a complicated subject that would take hours to break down, but I think the bottom line is that God has removed his active control of all actions on earth and delegated them to man—hence, our free will."

"Dan, you're saying God has removed his presence from earth?"

"I'm saying God has voluntarily and unilaterally ceased controlling man, and turned the planet over to us. So when bad things happen to good people, they're not the work of God, they're the work of Satan or natural occurrences which happen on a fallen world.

"We get to draw on God's power through invoking the written Scriptures that contain his promises, or covenants, to act on our behalf. That answers your claim that God is in control of everything. But getting back to free will and the need for us to use it for our own salvation... Christ told us when he was on earth, that God loves us and wants us to spend eternity with him, so he sent Christ to earth as a human to die and serve as our substitute for our sins. But salvation is an offer, not an automatic entitlement. We have to truly believe in Christ and desire a relationship with him. Christ's pledge to all humanity would have been false if God had already picked winners and losers."

Ben felt like his head might explode. It had to be the fatigue. "I'm not following."

"The Calvinists believe God preselects those who will be saved and calls them to him, while he lets the others march to their inevitable demise in hell. I think what causes the confusion is God knows both the present and the future simultaneously. He doesn't intervene on a real-time basis into people's lives, but I think he gives them every chance to believe throughout their lives while honoring free will. The bottom line, in my opinion, is that we ultimately choose where we go when we die."

"You're serious about these heaven and hell fictions, aren't you?" Ben asked. He felt his breathing get harder and his heart stutter. *Why does this upset me?* "It makes me wonder why a guy who caught spies and terrorists for a living is so wrapped up in what other people are doing in their personal lives."

"Love God and love thy neighbor—I care about people. They're the two main commandments Christians must follow. Because I love people, I'm bothered by the disastrous consequences of a person choosing to reject God—it's hardwired into my soul. I think existing in a place where God has no presence would be horrible beyond imagination." Dan shook his head.

Ben looked at him hard. "So you really believe in hell?"

Dan nodded. "Absolutely. Christ talked more about hell than heaven while he was on earth. It's clearly documented in the Bible. He was the ultimate authority figure to warn people."

"So your loving God created a place that is a very hot place where you feel pain—forever—right?" Ben's question reeked of his well-honed sarcasm.

"Right."

"So why would your wonderful God ever create such a place?"

"I was really troubled by that question. I couldn't believe God would actually let his creations suffer the way they do in hell. But after I listened to folks a lot more knowledgeable about the subject than me, I began to realize God isn't evil for creating hell, because it's ultimate justice for sinners who reject Christ out of their own free will. He gives us many, many chances to avoid it. It's up to us to accept him. How can

166

you expect God to let you into his home if you never made any effort to meet him?"

"Now we're talking about literally meeting God?" Ben snorted. "Do you have to make an appointment? Do you have to send your résumé ahead? What exactly are you talking about?"

Dan smiled. "I mean it in a supernatural sense. We don't understand the process, but we are born with a capability to connect with God through prayer and thought. Through continued prayer, we begin to develop a relationship with God. We communicate with him through our thoughts, like we think to ourselves. Our supernatural modem, if you will, is part of our spirit."

"You're saying it's some sort of telepathy that involves talking to yourself? Sounds like a description of mental illness to me. But even if I concede your theory about nonverbal communication with God is possible, you still can't explain why your good God would allow people to go to hell."

"I'll give you an example of how I think the process works. Let's say you're married right now, and you and your wife have a baby boy. You love and nurture your son; you give him all the necessities of life and more. As he grows, you make sure he gets a good education and has a good, stable home. You pay for his college, and he becomes a successful businessman. But as he matures and becomes wealthy, he begins to distance himself from you. He becomes hostile and resentful of what you've done for him, and he begins to tell others that his success was solely his own doing and you had nothing to do with it. In fact, he begins to attack you and your wife verbally, accusing you of being hypocrites and essentially being bad people. He starts drinking heavily and taking drugs on the side, physically abusing his own family, and you try to step in and help him. He not only rejects you, but he lashes out and posts notices on his Facebook page that he doesn't believe you're actually his father, and he claims his mother had an affair and he was the result. He goes on a warpath of insulting you, and in the meantime starts a life of crime and ends up in jail, losing his family—all the while being defiant and angrily rejecting you. Finally, despite all your attempts to help him, he rejects all contact from you."

Ben interjects, "Sounds like a real SOB."

"You've got that right. So when your son gets out of prison, he goes back on the streets and returns to a life of crime. One day your doorbell rings. You find your son standing at your front door, dressed like a street thug, and, with a swagger, he announces he's moving in. No apology, no explanation, no remorse for all he's done, and certainly no love for you as his father. Just arrogance and a demand: 'Let me in because I want to live in your house.' What would you do?"

"Slam the door."

"That's what I think God does. Imagine if a total stranger had knocked on your door and done the same thing. I believe God doesn't allow people in his house who have rejected him. Fair is fair, wouldn't you agree?"

Ben nodded. "I still don't see the direct connection with why we supposedly go to hell and have to suffer, though."

"The way I see it, your soul and spirit have to go somewhere when they detach from your body. And from what I can tell, there are two places they can go. My question is: Go where? The only authoritative work on the subject—the Bible—has clear descriptions of both places and how you get there."

"So anyone who doesn't acknowledge God's existence and ask for forgiveness from Jesus Christ is headed to hell—even if they lived life like a saint?"

"I don't know about the saint part because we all sin, but I'm pretty sure, even if you do good deeds in life, you'll be headed to hell if you refuse to accept the existence of God and the loving sacrifice that Jesus Christ made for you by dying on the cross. It's simple. Your ticket into heaven is your love for God and trust in Jesus."

"So, even if you're kind to other people, you'll go to hell if you don't love God?"

"I know that sounds kind of extreme, but yes, unless you have a true love for God, you'll go to hell."

"I take it he's answered your prayers? Did you hear a big booming voice?"

"I think God is much more subtle for most people; he drops the answers to your prayers in front of you, sometimes without being obvious."

Ben held an index finger to his lower lip and scowled. He was clearly not ready for Dan's stark warning. After a pause, he felt his heart rate calm down. He said, "I think you might have a problem with church attendance if you dwell on your macabre message—people want to hear happy stories about heaven. But let's say, for the sake of argument, that what you're saying is true. Then the church has a moral responsibility to sound the alarm, and I don't see that happening."

"You're absolutely right. The church should sound the alarm, but to be honest, you don't hear it discussed in church pulpits very often. Actually, some of the TV and radio evangelists are more active in addressing the topic head-on, but it is still rarely mentioned by most pastors and priests."

"Even though I don't buy them, your beliefs seem consistent. Why can't your clergy get the warning out about hell and convince people to believe?"

"Some avoid it because it's a turnoff, and some sort of sugarcoat it. I think a lot of pastors shy away from talking about hell because of what you described; they don't want to scare people away with fire and brimstone."

"You're on to something. Maybe there's hope for you yet," Ben said, getting to his feet and stretching his arms above his head.

"One of the most important messages is that God pursues us with his unrelenting goodness and love, and he also gives us the power to reject him. It's your choice; you're completely free to do whatever you want. He offers you a gift. You have to make the effort to accept it, and if you don't, you'll spend eternity with Satan and his mob."

Ben sat silently, staring straight ahead. When it was his time, where would *he go*? After a minute of stewing, he turned to Dan. "Why are you so wedded to the belief that hell is a place of physical torment?"

"Two reasons. First, it's clearly stated in the Bible. Second, that's what some of the near-death experience witnesses report happened to them when they went to hell. I wish it weren't true, but I can't rule it out when I keep reading accounts of witnesses who claim it is. What made me start to think that some of the reported experiences might be true was when I was digging through the Bible looking for some information, and came across a passage that described almost perfectly an experience I had recently read about on an NDE website. A witness, who took the time to fill out a questionnaire for no money and no recognition, reported that he fell into a pit and was covered in worms during his NDE. He said the worms had claws and teeth. I was in Isaiah at the time and read 14:11—it described someone being brought down to the grave and having maggots spread out beneath them and being covered in worms. The witness made no mention of the Bible in his questionnaire and didn't report he was a Christian in the section that asks about religious faith, so I doubt he fabricated his account only to get a Bible verse slid into the database through deception. It's possible, but I doubt it."

"If what you're saying is true about the reports, I have to agree—they shouldn't be rejected out of hand. Interpreting them the way you do is another matter. But go on," Ben said, settling against the back of his seat.

"I think others can't reconcile their concept of God with the thought that he created hell. Like I said, I can't stand the thought of hell, but I accept its existence since it's God's will that it exists. I've come to realize that God is ultimately fair and just, and he has done everything he can do to keep man out of hell, while not interfering with our free will."

"You can't resist the temptation to give a sermon, can you? Why don't you simply describe what you've learned and leave out the evangelical spin?" Ben asked. "Your sermonizing is falling on deaf ears."

"I may sound like I'm preaching, but I'm describing a problem—hell—and a solution—salvation. No value judgment and no pressure—take or leave it, and live the way you want to live."

Ben shook his head and stared at the floor. Dan had hit a nerve ... but what was it about? He closed his eyes. His turmoil had to be related to his fatigue.

"Ben. Why don't you call your daughter and let her know you're on your way?" Dan asked softly.

Ben dismissed his question with a wave of his hand. "Like I said, I had to do it this way. Our rift is too deep to fix on the phone."

"Yeah, but we're talking common courtesy here," Dan said. "I can't believe you're doing this. Do you really have her number?"

Ben laughed. "Yes. I had my grad assistant track her down on the Web."

"Ah, that's right. You've been spying on her. Welcome to my world."

# CHAPTER TWELVE

## *The Rescue Party*

A flash of yellow light pierced the darkened concourse windows and bathed the side of Dan's face with a pulsating illumination.

Startled out of what was becoming a deep sleep, he felt a strong vibration course through the terminal floor as a caravan of heavy emergency trucks sprayed salt on the icy runways—the first sign of activity since the storm had begun. The power had gone off again, and now the temperature in the concourse was noticeably colder. Dan got up to see the taillights of the last truck rumble past.

*Can't believe this has happened*, Dan thought. He looked over and noticed only Ben's scuffed briefcase sat in his seat. He had obviously left again during Dan's nap.

Dan grabbed the case and shouldered his backpack. Time to find a restroom. He walked carefully through the sleeping masses and found a men's lavatory with the faint glow of an emergency light outlining the entrance. As he walked into the shadowy entrance, the lights came back on and momentarily blinded him. He squinted as his eyes adjusted and he stepped up to a urinal.

Gazing ahead absentmindedly, he heard the sound of someone else come into the restroom and shuffle to a far urinal.

As Dan turned to leave, lost in thought, he slowed and stopped. There stood Stan Crofton at the end urinal.

*I'll keep walking—maybe he won't notice me.*

"Dan!"

*Too late!* Dan felt nauseated. He had hoped never to see the guy again and here he was, right in front of him. Dan waited a moment, and then turned to face his old nemesis. Dan heard Connie's words in his mind: *"... maybe you need to pray again about forgiving him."*

Stan washed his hands, and snatched a paper towel and dried them. "Surprised to see you here. I thought you put yourself out to pasture."

The cynicism in Stan's voice was so thick it hit Dan like a noxious odor. *This guy hasn't changed a bit—still as arrogant as ever.*

"No, I'm still kicking. What brings you to Charlotte?" Dan's voice was equally strained.

"Oh, just passin' through. Had a meeting downtown and now I'm headed back to DC. I've got a small consulting company—something to keep me busy. You know, the typical beltway bandit outfit. How are Connie and the girls?"

Crofton's voice oozed insincerity and his facial expression of a faintly disguised smirk said it all. After all these years, they still hadn't buried the hatchet. Dan didn't want to prolong the agony, but he was cornered. And perhaps it was time. Didn't he tell Ben about loving his neighbor?

Dan smiled, though he knew it was far from his best one. "They're all fine. How are Jean and the kids? Still in Annapolis?"

"Everybody's doing great. We've kept the old place—can't move now, with the kids still in college and Jean's job."

Dan nodded. "I see you're trapped here like the rest of us."

"Yeah, this is some storm. I won't get out of here until noon. My schedule's shot now."

Dan shook his head. Same old all-about-Stan. "Hasn't done much for anyone's schedule, Stan."

The lights flickered and went out again. "Guess that's a signal for me to get back to my gate," Crofton said, and walked toward the faint outline of the exit door.

Dan felt like he needed a shower. Another typical encounter—all pleasantries to hide the animosity bubbling under the surface. *This is no way to act. It's time to practice what I preach and extend the olive branch; this lying to each other is wrong.*

***

Dan struggled with his conflicted thoughts all the way back to his seat. Ben was already in his familiar perch, with a newspaper opened.

"You don't look so good—see a ghost? Oh, that's right. There are no ghosts, only angels and demons." He chuckled.

"I saw someone I'd rather forget."

"An old girlfriend you spurned?"

"A lot worse. An old coworker who almost ruined my career."

175

"Sounds serious. He obviously didn't succeed. What happened?" Ben asked, setting the paper aside.

"Another long story—I don't like talking about it."

"I'm shocked. I thought you loved talking about your cloak-and-dagger world."

"This was personal, not just professional."

Dan decided how much to say while Ben waited silently.

Glancing at his watch, Dan thought, *Sleep will be elusive at best—why not talk it out?*

Dan handed Ben his briefcase, then stowed his backpack under the seat and began his story. "This guy tried to ruin my career behind my back. It started when we were overseas. I had a CI Operations Squad and he had a CI Collections Squad in the same field office. One day I get called into the SAC's office—our special agent-in-charge. He tells me point-blank that an internal inquiry—a 2B, as we call it—had been opened on me and my squad members. We were suspected of pocketing operational funds and writing them off on phony payments to assets. The allegations were made by an anonymous caller to the inspector general's hotline. I considered the SAC both my boss and a friend, and I was shocked. There was nothing he could do."

"You weren't fired, were you?"

"No. I was temporarily relieved of my duties and all of our active counterintelligence ops were stopped, and two ops ended up being ruined due to the delay. After three weeks of digging through our files, auditing our expenses, talking to our assets, and interviewing almost the entire field office, the IG team gave us a clean bill of health."

"Did they go back and investigate the anonymous caller?"

"Not that I know of. I didn't have proof, but I knew who did it. The timing was key. The investigation came right before a promotion board and surprise, surprise, the Collections Squad Leader got promoted and I didn't, even though my squad ran rings around his. IG investigations aren't supposed to be a factor in promotions, but they always are. It took me years to clear my reputation."

"I wouldn't be very happy with that person either. You obviously overcame the setback, though," Ben said quietly.

"I did, and in fact, I'd about forgotten the whole mess when a friend called me one day. He overheard Crofton bragging in a bar to a bunch of DEA agents that they shouldn't worry about the competition when it comes to promotion boards—that's why they made IG hotlines! He all but confessed he'd made the call, my friend said. All this because the guy wanted to make me look bad so he'd get promoted."

"I would have killed the bastard," Ben snarled.

"I thought about it, but that's where it ended. I had a source at the time, an explosives expert, who volunteered to rig any car I wanted with explosives. I actually thought about it for a few seconds … for the pleasure of it. Crofton and I went our separate ways, and I only saw him in passing at our headquarters. He could tell by the way I acted that I must have found out what he did. He avoided me like the plague after that, but never changed his attitude."

"Like I said, I would have killed the bastard." Ben paused. "Oh, by the way, I found an article in the paper that might interest you." He ruffled the pages with a flurry for effect.

Dan was mildly curious. "Yes?"

"Harvard has been studying a scrap of papyrus from the fourth century. Seems your beloved Jesus may have been married."

"I've read the articles—they surface off and on. If I remember correctly, a lot of experts have been skeptical of the piece and some say it's an outright forgery."

"If it's not, doesn't that destroy the grand theory about your Messiah? Wasn't he supposed to be God in a human body, completely sinless, removed from man because of his holy state—and now they think he was married?"

"Even the Harvard researcher who presented the specimen is skeptical."

"You know you'd have a better chance of convincing people there's a God if you'd dispense with the Jesus nonsense. You'd even be in synch with the synagogues if you stuck to what we were taught—worshiping God because he supposedly created the universe. Why complicate the story with an eccentric rabbi who could do magic tricks?"

"It's the truth! And now that you mention it, that's why the acceptance of the reality of heaven and hell is so critical. Without God's judgment and hell, Christ isn't necessary from a human's perspective. But since hell exists, he's not only necessary, he's our one-man rescue party. I don't mean to diminish the magnificence of Christ in any way, but the simple fact is that Christ came to earth to lead us to heaven, save us from hell, and neuter Satan. Christ didn't come to earth to create a religion; he came to give us emergency evacuation instructions from a fallen world that Adam and Eve left us stranded in. He went down with the ship in our place. He died so we could use his lifeboat, so to speak—we have to accept his loving grace and climb into the boat he left us and we'll be safe. Ignore his selfless act of sacrifice and we go down with the ship too."

Ben laughed. "You have to make references to the navy, don't you?"

"It comes naturally, and I'm not the first to use the nautical metaphor. But really, the critical aspect of Christ's time on earth was not just his life of teachings, miracles, and his execution, but his resurrection. God used him to pay for our sins—the laws of supernatural justice established by God were satisfied. Remember the concept of salvation by grace?"

"How could I forget?"

Dan nodded. "That's why I used to get upset with the church's avoidance of addressing near-death experiences. I remember watching a Christian cable channel video that talked about salvation. It was well done overall, and it basically talked about the different views regarding what happens to us when we die. But then at the end, it asked the viewer, 'Why take a chance? You'll never know what will happen to you until you die, and then it's too late. Only Jesus came back from the grave, and you need to accept him,' or something like that."

"And ...."

Dan smiled at the memory. "I was yelling at the TV, 'What do you mean, we'll never know what happens to us until we die?' We have thousands of eyewitnesses who can tell us a lot about what happens—and more every day. God is basically providing us with signs and wonders through resuscitated NDE eyewitnesses, and the church is treating them like they don't exist!"

"What did you mean; you used to be upset with the church?"

"When I started to think about the complexity of the subject, I realized why the church can't do a wholesale endorsement of the validity of NDEs."

"And why's that?" Ben asked while crossing his arms above his belly.

"They don't have the capability to vet the various self-identified NDE and OBE witnesses, and they run the risk of endorsing a fabricator or someone who's undergone a deceptive experience. The whole subject area is a minefield for the church."

"No church has ever presented an NDE eyewitness?"

"Some have, but on a limited basis. They're usually people that the church knows and have had some form of vetting. A few well-known Christian NDE and OBE eyewitnesses do go out on the lecture circuit and speak at churches about their visits to heaven and hell and their encounters with Jesus, but the number of churches affected is relatively small. I still think it's an important field of study that the church should try to understand better and use on a careful basis. After all, following his death and resurrection, Christ made a point of visiting people who knew him so he could prove in the flesh that he had been raised from the dead. The Christian church should be attempting to meet the same burden of proof today with carefully selected NDE witnesses."

"Didn't Christ have a near-death experience?"

"No. He was put to death and wasn't revived by a doctor. God *resurrected* him."

"At least, according to legend."

"It's not legend. If it were, the story of Christ would have been embellished over time and made a lot more glamorous and uplifting than it was. Who would think up the horrific events that led up to Christ's crucifixion and pass them off as the final glorious days of the Son of God on earth? I mean, really. A Jewish carpenter turned self-taught rabbi who led a bunch of ragtag followers, one of whom betrayed him for money and one who denied knowing him at his greatest hour of need. The Son of God who was horribly beaten and then nailed to a cross—and yet he didn't lift a finger to fight back while Roman soldiers spat in his face and mashed a crown of thorns into his scalp. What kind of God is that? Who would be inspired by such a story? But his disciples were, because it happened. Once they saw Jesus alive again, their worlds changed forever. Some died terrible deaths at the hands of executioners when upholding their faith, yet they never renounced their belief in Jesus. Why let yourself be tortured to death for a phony story?"

"Okay, I'll concede that Christ could have lived and died as advertised, but it still doesn't answer the fundamental question of how a good God could send his people to hell. I know you say God doesn't know people who reject him, but God could change them in an instant and save them."

Dan asked, "Ben, can I force you to like something?"

"Not really."

"Then I surely can't make you love something, can I?"

"No. I have to concede you can't."

"Your answer is at the heart of why we decide where we go when our body dies. God truly gave us free will—with no strings attached. For God to give you the priceless gift of being able to love others and to receive love in return, he also had to give you the power to reject love and to deny it to others. Either we're marionettes here on earth or we truly are free beings."

"What a crude, brutal way to create a universe. Why not make everything perfect and beautiful?"

"God did, originally, with Adam and Eve, but once Satan got into the mix he destroyed the paradise. I also think that, more to your point, you have to have contrasts so you can perceive differences. We have to experience hot to understand cold. We have to have imperfect to understand and appreciate perfection. We'll never fully understand why God created the universe the way he did, until we stand in God's presence and connect with his loving spirit."

"Even if I were to accept your explanation about Christ and heaven and hell, I'm repelled by the very thought of it all. No wonder the Christian faith is dying."

"It's not dying, but the number of Christian households in America is declining."

"I'll give you credit. Your faith seems genuine—a rare commodity these days," said Ben with a rueful smile.

Dan settled himself into the seat in an attempt to get comfortable again. "You're right, I have faith. But I've developed it the hard way."

"Everyone makes mistakes, or sins, as you put it."

"True, but the earlier in life you have your MTB—your moment of true belief—the fewer people you're likely to hurt along the way—and in the end, that's important. Living life with Christ's energy and love connected to you can make a huge difference in your making good decisions and saving yourself and a lot of other people a lot of pain."

"Sounds like you're crying over spilled milk."

"I'm not. I'm stating fact. When you're filled with love, you create a lot less misery in the world."

"All right. I concede there's a thread of logic to your argument. I can't find any obvious holes in your case about people sending themselves to hell, but give me time—I'll find something. You're addressing biblical concepts I haven't had time to research."

"I wouldn't wait too long, Ben. You never know when your time here on earth will end."

"Nice try, my friend, but I'm not ready to join your camp. Besides, I'm running out of steam."

"I'm almost there myself. By the way, I was wondering, why now?" Dan asked with pointed directness. "Why visit your daughter now, after all these years? She's still married to the same man."

Dan's question hit Ben at a vulnerable moment. As if to relieve the pain of a pinched nerve, he shifted in his seat and spoke in a flat, hushed tone. "At the beginning of the fall semester last year, a gal walked into one of my intro courses. She could have been Ruth's twin. She looked exactly like Ruth did when she was about eighteen or nineteen—right down to the way she fixed her hair and dressed.

"I couldn't take my eyes off her—it was embarrassing. About halfway through the class, I started to feel an intense sense of regret and guilt. It was like I woke up from a deep sleep. I started to miss my daughter—I wanted to see her again. That started the process that led me to being here today."

"Is that when you had your grad assistant track your daughter down?"

"Yeah. I knew I had to reconnect with her. It was my fault we had a falling out, and now it's my responsibility to make amends. She's my flesh and blood and I'm not getting any younger."

"Did you ever talk to the student?"

"I never saw her again. I assume she dropped after the first class. I don't take attendance, so I have no idea who she was."

"You know when you told me you'd be able to patch things up with your daughter if you saw her face-to-face, I thought that idea didn't stand a chance. But after hearing why you want to see her, I think you can pull it off. You've had a change of heart. And you know when it comes to God, that's all he wants too."

"You never give up."

"I never will."

# CHAPTER THIRTEEN

## *Warmth of the Soul*

Three bottles of energy drink landed on the counter with a thud, jolting the drowsy cashier at the twenty-four-hour minimart.

"Gimme a pack of menthols too."

"Anything else?" asked the middle-aged man as he rang up the items while covering a yawn.

"Nah. Any all-night restaurants around here?" the gaunt young man asked, handing over a credit card to the cashier.

The cashier looked warily at the man's shaking hand and retrieved the card. "Not anything close by; most everything's closed. You're the first customer we've had in a couple of—" The cashier frowned at the machine in front of him. "Sir, your credit card's been declined."

"Run it again. It's good."

The cashier ran the card again. "Sir, it's still coming back as declined."

"Wait a minute." Richie stomped out the door in a huff.

"Gimme your purse," Richie grunted as he pulled open Joy's door.

"You know where it is; right where you threw it."

He leaned into the cab and pulled out a tan leather handbag from under the seat and snatched two twenty-dollar bills from the wallet inside.

"What's the matter? Did Daddy cut off your credit cards?" Joy snapped at him, with tears in her eyes.

"Keep your mouth closed if you want somethin' to drink. I'll be back—sit still."

Richie picked his way carefully over the slick pavement and laid a crumpled twenty-dollar bill on the counter. After grabbing his drinks and pocketing the change, he inched his way back to the pickup and heaved the brown plastic bag into Joy's lap. Both remained silent as he slammed the door shut.

Instead of starting the truck, he slowly leaned his forehead against the steering wheel while lightly pounding it with his clenched fists. He fought back tears and closed his eyes.

"I told you this was coming, Richie, but you wouldn't listen, would you? Now look at you—you're strung out and broke. You've got to get cleaned up, babe, and get your life back together." She sniffed and choked back a sob. "And it needs to be now. I need you. And your baby needs you too. Please, Richie, listen to me."

He lifted his head and swiped a few tears with the sleeve of his jacket. He nodded, then looked at her. "I will, I will. I just need time. Once I talk to Dad, he'll help me get back on my feet. I'll get through this, you'll see. It'll be like old times, when we were good."

The woman shook her head, the tears welling." What happened to us? Why the drugs, baby?" she asked softly.

He shook his head and turned to face the window. He started the truck and adjusted the heater. "I don't know. I'm lost. You know, my dad had big plans for me. Go to college, get a government job like him, buy the big, impressive house. But then what? I don't think my father loves anything but his lousy job. The mighty, all-powerful Stan Crofton! Behold and beware. He can't tell the truth from the lies anymore, but that's probably a benefit of the job. I *never* wanted to be him. I *never* wanted his life."

She watched him stare out the frozen windshield. "What *do* you want, Richie?"

He turned to her and forced a smile. *I want you. I want our baby. I want to get clean and have a normal life ....* He let his tears fall as he spoke his answer. "I don't know, Joy. I want to stop shaking, I want to stop being afraid—I want to be a good father and a good husband." He cleared his throat. "If I can't reach my father before he leaves town, none of that will matter. I owe way too much money to these people. When the storm passes, I'm a dead man."

"You could go to the police. Let them help us with this."

He shook his head. "Are you crazy? They'll put me in jail, and what do I do then? Some stupid public defender will let them throw away the key. One less strung-out addict to worry about."

Joy studied his face a long time, and then nodded as a single tear ran down her cheek. "Will you take me home now? You need to do whatever you're going to do, but I need to go home. Me and the baby don't need all this stress."

He reached for the bag with the drinks in it. "I got you two without any caffeine," he said. "The other one is for me. I can't take you home. I'm not sure it's safe ... and I need you with me. More than you know."

She reached out to stroke his gaunt, unshaven face, then sighed and let her hand drop into her lap. She blinked back tears and looked away.

"Buckle up, baby. We're going to try the airport one more time."

The acceleration of the truck pushed her back in the seat as they headed into the wintery darkness. The truck's headlights cut cone-shaped paths of brightness into the diminishing droplets of sleet.

\*\*\*

In the terminal, Ben dropped into his seat at the departure gate, jarring Dan, who was leaning on his backpack and trying to sleep.

"They must have reopened some of the roads. I saw the same pickup drive by the front of the terminal again. Must be trying to pick someone up or something. The roads are still real bad, but some must be getting passable."

Dan shifted awkwardly as he tried to find a comfortable spot on the firm vinyl seat. Drowsy but unable to fall back asleep, he fished around blindly in his backpack for a magazine and felt his earphones. Although still groggy from a lack of deep sleep, he plugged the earphones into his phone and scanned his playlist with one eye open until he found his favorite album. After hitting Play, he leaned back with his eyes closed, gently nodding his head to the rhythm of the song.

"Tapping into your direct line to heaven?" Ben asked.

Dan opened his eyes and turned to Ben with his eyebrows raised. "Music relaxes me. I never travel without it."

"I thought you'd be listening to Bible verses, maybe something narrated by Billy Graham or Charlton Heston."

Dan chuckled. "Hate to disappoint you—it's just music." He noticed Ben was fully awake.

"I'm shocked. You actually do something not connected to the Promised Land?"

Dan made a mock grimace and shook his head. "You had to get me goin' again, didn't you?"

"Ah, I can't sleep and I'm too tired to read. Sad to say, my eyes aren't as strong as they used to be. Besides, this conversation has been fascinating. I'd like to hear what else you have swirling around in that gray matter of yours."

"All right, you asked for it." Dan hit Stop on his phone and neatly folded his earphones before turning to face Ben.

"I think music has power. It speaks to our soul in a physical sense, and it can heal or harm our body. I never realized until recently how much music has affected my life. I may not look the type now, but I used to play in a rock band when I was younger."

"Really? Somehow I can't picture you as a headbanger— you're too establishment-looking." Ben smiled easily.

Dan laughed. "Yeah, I wouldn't fit in with the rock-and-roll crowd today, but I didn't always look like this. Music was actually my profession for a few years, but I quit the band when I got tired of playing in smoke-filled bars. I never lost my love for music, though; it gets in your blood."

"Is that so? What did you play?"

"Guitar. I picked it up in the '60s when rock music became big. My friends and I all wanted to be big rock stars, but somehow that didn't happen—go figure, right? But I'll tell you one thing. Groups like the Beatles changed my life forever, and so did a lot of the Motown and soul bands like James Brown. I was totally immersed in music when I was growing up."

Ben nodded. "We all were to some extent, and you're right about the quick rise of rock and roll being a shift in our culture. You could make the argument that it had one of the biggest impacts on us baby boomers who were still under the influence of our parents—the so-called Greatest Generation. I don't know if they were the greatest, but they sure were the most prudish and rigid, I'll bet. I think rock and roll liberated us and gave us a freer way of life. It spawned a counterculture that still exists today."

"I look at rock music differently now," Dan said. "I think it did move our culture in a specific direction, but not a good one. Some Christians actually believe rock and roll was inspired by Satan to further his master plan of pulling man away from God. And they might be right, I don't know. I think some rock is fine, but something happened when it began to evolve into different genres that had a malevolent feel to them. If you ask me, some of today's rock and rap and hip-hop are damaging the moral fiber of our society."

"Oh, please! That statement surprises me, you being a professional protector of freedom. Should we go back to burning books and records in front of city hall?"

"No, of course not. I believe in freedom of expression, but I also think something negative happened to our culture in the

'60s, and I think music played a part. I'll never forget the first time I heard Jimi Hendrix. 'Purple Haze' completely blew me away. I'd never heard anything like it. It was the tone quality of his guitar—that distortion—and the structure of his songs. Now, when I look back I think his music hit my soul like a corrosive chemical. It sounded great then, but there was a dark quality about it that I never thought about until I started looking at some of the Christian commentaries on rock that have been done over the years."

"So Jimi Hendrix made music from hell?"

Dan shrugged. "Let me ask you something, Ben. As an academic, what's your opinion of the effect of literature on the mind and fabric of a young person? If all a student read was comic books, would you consider him well educated?"

Ben laughed. "Of course not. To be well educated, one must be well read. I mean, a wide variety of literature would be needed to allow a student to develop a well-rounded world view."

"All right. Now, if a student tended to read only one type of literature—let's say, all the works written by Adolf Hitler—do you think that would impact his or her world view, as you put it? And if so, how?" Dan asked.

"Of course it would. In time, the student would be a Jew-hater and probably a powerfully disillusioned student. Unfortunately, we are seeing that on campuses all over the world these days."

"Music has the same ability to influence, though it is much more subtle, I think. To use a term from my world—subversive. Back to Hendrix. It wasn't merely his music; it was what he started. Everyone wanted that distorted sound for their guitar, including me. But it also brought with it a quality that hit you on a more primordial level. Our heartbeats raced, our minds literally stopped mid-thought until all that was left was a raging emotion.

"I actually think Satan could have inspired rock to give him a new channel to use to influence people's souls on a large scale without being obvious. After Hendrix and other groups made it big, you had a lot more songs about sex, drugs, revolution, and just plain evil. I think the end result has been that today we have music genres like death metal—pure spiritual sewage."

"He wasn't alone; there were lots of groups like his," Ben replied.

"You're right. The Stones were one of the first to use distortion when they made 'Satisfaction,' but Hendrix brought it to a whole new level. And, some argue that Hendrix's music was an expression of his own torment and questions about the world, not a call to action. I suspect it was both. Now we have heavy metal with satanic lyrics, stage sets right out of hell, and demonic album art. I also think it's interesting that we now have some rap and hip-hop that have blatant evil messages which reach an entirely different demographic. But it all started during our generation. I don't think it's a coincidence that the Church of Satan was founded in 1966—right around the time rock became mainstream."

Ben nodded. "All right, I'll concede that 'I Can't Get No Satisfaction' probably wasn't inspired by the deity. For that matter, I can't think of any groups from their era that were."

"I can think of one group right off the bat. The Beach Boys. I know some will point out that the late Dennis Wilson, the group's original drummer, palled around with Charles

Manson for a short time, but I think some of their songs speak for themselves."

"Really? Aren't those guys all dead?"

"Actually, some of the remaining members are still active, though I'm not sure what difference that makes. Many of the old rockers are now dead, too. The Beach Boys produced music with a spiritual quality to it. 'God Only Knows' and others songs, like 'Heaven' and 'That's Why God Made the Radio,' are pretty straightforward—they mention God in a positive light. But more than that, their beautiful harmonies definitely soothe the soul and warm the heart."

"How do you get from Bible student to music critic?"

"I picked up on it when I started to study the rise of Satanism in America, which, by the way, is something a small group in the law enforcement community keeps an eye on. There is little else with the power to fuel revolution and terrorism—even homegrown terrorism—like the dark religions."

Ben's eyes opened wide. "You mean you guys really do track what religions are doing in America? Sounds to me a lot like Hitler's time."

"We looked at Islamic fundamentalist jihadists from an antiterrorism perspective, but not any of the occult-based religions unless they were implicated in a specific case. But some private researchers do. You have to understand, Ben, there is a growing number of Christian scholars who track patterns and trends in society—many with a biblical and a supernatural world view. All of the influences on the human being are important. There's horrible evil done in the name of one so-called god or another. As a Jew, you know what I'm talking about."

Ben nodded.

"I kept finding articles that focused on the growing trend of artists using occult and satanic imagery and messages in their music. I never paid any attention to it when I was younger, but I was surprised when I actually read the lyrics of some of the Stones' songs, like 'Sympathy for the Devil,' which some claim is the anthem for the Church of Satan. The more I looked, the more I found albums like *Their Satanic Majesties Request* and *The Rolling Stones – Live 666*."

"That's show biz," Ben said quickly. "They have to have shock value to get people's attention and stand out from the crowd. It all gets back to money; they have to find a way to sell their songs. I bet they don't have a clue about Satanism."

Dan said, "That's what I once thought too, but I don't think so now. Even if the Stones were dumb kids back then trying to be cool, there's way too much of it in today's music and videos to dismiss it all as trying to be different. When I started looking at rock and pop, I counted more than thirty groups or artists, ranging from heavy metal to hip-hop and rap that either have 666 somewhere on their album cover or a reference to Lucifer or the occult in their songs, and I only scratched the surface."

"You yourself said you never take anything at face value. Why are you taking these singers and their songs so literally? They're just wannabes."

"As a Christian, I take it seriously because they're influencing our kids in a negative way. They're actually praising Satan in songs, and I think the spiritual damage to some people is not only obvious, but real. I've got grandchildren I care about. So do you. I can't afford to wear those blinders anymore."

"If you think their music's so harmful, don't listen to it."

"You're right about having a choice. I *don't* listen. But a lot of kids without supervision or with parents who don't know—or care—get subjected to this stuff every day, and by the time they're older, they're conditioned to accept it. Plus, there's peer pressure. You know how a particular style of music or entertainment can gradually become intertwined into the social fabric of a culture until it's accepted as normal. You're a sociology professor."

"I'd have to agree that if I did believe in Satan, I'd probably conclude that Satan and his dark kingdom may have deliberately used music and entertainment to influence the world," Ben said with a frown.

Dan nodded. "I suspect his goal has been to condition people to treat him as a benign entity. Abortion, genocide, even euthanasia for our elders are now things that barely get noticed anymore. Once we reach a certain level of tolerance and ultimate acceptance of evil in our society, I think the end is near. I don't think God will stand by and let the process continue."

Ben wrinkled his nose as though exasperated. "I told you—it's a marketing tactic. The music may not be very wholesome, but what is, these days?"

"There is some uplifting entertainment out there, like classical and some Christian music, and other types too, but you have to search for it. Rap and hip-hop are everywhere on radio and TV, but you don't see any cable channels devoted to symphonic music—at least not where I live. I first started looking at the current entertainment scene after Bill O'Reilly ran a segment on a Beyoncé and Jay-Z music video that showed Beyoncé acting like a prostitute and finally being killed in a car that Jay-Z set on fire. O'Reilly's contention was that a multimillionaire like Beyoncé should be producing positive material for her young and impressionable audience and not sexually suggestive stuff that will harm kids. He approached it as a cultural problem, and I think he's right. I also think it's a symptom of a spiritual problem."

"O'Reilly? That loudmouthed crackpot?" Ben's lips formed into a smirk.

"He tells it like it is," Dan said. "I don't always agree with him, but he tackles big issues that others in the media ignore."

"I don't waste my time with TV, particularly that kind of drivel. I know you see God in everything, but O'Reilly?" Ben shook his head and folded his arms across his chest.

"You should watch him and judge for yourself. Now that you mention it, O'Reilly is one of a very few secular TV personalities who actually states on national television that he prays for people."

"Halleluiah! He's playing to the Bible-thumpers like you."

Dan laughed. "He's not playing to anyone; he's being honest."

"So that explains his vendetta against hip-hop artists?" Ben asked, his voice on the edge of a snarl.

"I don't think it's a vendetta. It's a challenge to the rich and powerful who are harming kids and potentially doing a lot worse. He's exposing evil, and for that he should be commended. Others, like Gov. Mike Huckabee, have also made some of the same points."

"You make it sound like these artists are casting magic spells over the audience."

"Some would say that's exactly what they're doing because of the power of the symbols they use in their videos and photos. I'd say, at the very least, their music conditions their audience to tolerate and eventually accept the satanic and occult as cool. When I started to dig into the material of Beyoncé and Jay-Z, I noticed they wear clothes that have symbols or sayings from the Ordo Templi Orientis, a cultlike organization created by the late Aleister Crowley, who was a self-professed Satanist.

"Beyoncé's photos speak for themselves; she's worn an outfit with the occult deity Baphomet on it, and she's also been photographed wearing a Goat of Mendes ring and a T-shirt with a pentagram. They also flash the triangle with their hands onstage sometimes, a symbol from the OTO and an alleged occult group, the Illuminati. Jay-Z's made a halfhearted attempt to downplay the alleged connection, but his songs like 'Lucifer' and 'Empire State of Mind' speak for themselves. When you sing that Jesus can't save you and your life starts when the church ends, you can't take that back."

Ben threw his arms up in frustration. "You haven't listened to a word I've said. Even if their hand signals are from some sort of secret society, as you claim, and their lyrics are heretical, it's a gimmick, and it's not going to lead people to the devil."

"I disagree. Symbols convey meanings which we process on a subconscious level. They send a specific message to the young and impressionable—that Satan and his demons are hip—and by extension, God is not. If they'd been making the sign of the cross in a respectful way, they'd get a huge reaction—almost certainly negative. Watch the hip-hop videos for yourself. Some are full of pentagrams and witchcraft imagery, and some even have scenes where churches or

Christlike images are desecrated. Even if it's a gimmick, it's the wrong message to send to the young, who blindly imitate people they admire. I think the actual result is that it erodes a person's belief in God, if they have any faith to begin with. Worse, the celebrities literally become objects of worship for the kids."

"Idol worship has been part of cultures for centuries. We all have our idols. If you follow sports teams or celebrities, then you probably have them too."

Dan said, "I'm past that stage. One of the biggest benefits of being a student of the Bible is that it helps you put things in perspective. I'm more concerned about eternity than being entertained. I care about people and the harm that may be inflicted on them."

Ben smiled. "I have to admit your motives are noble, but even if I concede that the music industry is darkening the souls of the audience in the name of the almighty buck, I don't think you can prove its deliberate spiritual subversion."

"I do. Look at some of the past Grammys—prime-time network shows. In 2012, Nicki Minaj performed as someone possessed by an alter ego named Roman, went through a confession onstage in a way that mocked Catholicism, then underwent a simulated exorcism, and finally levitated while an altar boy prayed between the legs of a dancer.

"Two years later, at the 56th Grammys—Beyoncé opened the show with a pole dance that a stripper would do in a gentlemen's club, and then Katy Perry performed what many called a witchcraft ritual, complete with dancers in demon costumes gyrating in front of flames. Big stars like Katy Perry know what they're doing. In 2015, AC/DC opened the Grammys with 'Rock Or Bust' and 'Highway to Hell' while the audience wore lit red devil horns, and Madonna continued the theme with a song that had a stage full of dancers wearing demonic-looking headgear with horns. The imagery was obvious and clearly deliberate."

"Sorry, my friend, but I think you're making a mountain out of a molehill."

"Maybe so, but I believe inspiration for music and video content comes from the soul and affects the souls of others. NDE witnesses report that music is a big part of heaven. If both God and the demonic have access to our souls while we're here on earth, then music and entertainment can be used for good or evil. You eventually become what you listen to, or, as the old saying goes, if you lie down with dogs long enough, you're gonna get fleas."

"All right, even if I concede your point that entertainers put satanic themes in their music to have a specific effect, you don't know why. Maybe their producers made them do it. You still can't prove your theory that they're willingly serving Satan."

"I can't prove they believe in Satan, but I can take them at their word. Some musicians have clearly stated that they've sold their souls to the devil to become big stars."

"Oh, really. More show-biz nonsense."

"Okay," said Dan, with a shrug. "Then people are not influenced by what they read or see, either. They aren't influenced by the behaviors they see in their parents or peers, right?"

Ben frowned. "Of course we're influenced by those things. I've seen the studies about the impact of music on mentally ill patients, as well as prenatal and developing infants. Scientists have proven there is a consequence.

They've measured it. But what I'm arguing is that people can be ignorant about what they are doing, too. How much truth exists in any kind of marketing, anyway? This is another example of hype, my friend."

"It's more. Do the research and you'll see," Dan said. "I'll give you an example. When Ed Bradley interviewed Bob Dylan on *60 Minutes* some years ago, Dylan confessed that he made a deal in order to become famous. When Ed asked him who he made a deal with, he said 'the Chief Commander on this Earth and in the World we can't see.' I don't think he was talking about God."

"Nobody listens to Dylan anymore; he's a has-been."

"There are a lot of others too. I started to look into some of the current stars and was surprised to see how many have stated in public forums or in their songs that they sold their soul to Satan. Big names like Kanye West, Katy Perry, Beyoncé, and Eminem."

"You're persistent. I'll give you that much credit, Dan, but you still don't understand. They're just trying to get attention and it's obvious it has worked. I doubt if any of them have any kind of affinity for *anything* spiritual."

"If they don't, then why mention it?" Dan said. "You can shock people and get their attention a whole lot of ways. Seems strange to me that so many specifically mention the devil."

"We still have some latent puritanical roots in our culture, Dan. The best way to stand out is to attack the pillars of society. Plus, people change. Even if they do dabble in the occult now, they'll probably grow out of it. I listened to the Stones and the Beatles when I was young, and I don't think it had any effect on me at all—it was a phase in my socialization. Now I listen to classical music occasionally, so what does that make me?"

"A lover of the arts. Classical music stimulates intellectual creativity—a good thing. One way or another, though, music that stimulates the soul can either heal or harm. Some studies have shown that teens who listen to music with sexually degrading messages are more apt to be promiscuous at an early age. There's also a new medical field called music therapy. Hospitals and clinics now hire college-educated specialists who perform specific types of music to speed healing and achieve specific positive outcomes in patients. Science and medicine have recognized the power of music."

Ben clasped his hands and said, "You've finally made a claim you might be able to back up. I'm not familiar in great detail with the field of music therapy, but I've read some articles and studies. I get your point."

"And I think I'm finally getting through to you." Dan laughed. "You're getting soft."

"I'm willing to concede a point if it's true. You're wasting your time with your war on music, though."

"I disagree. Christians have to take a stand and call out evil when they see it. One of the biggest sins we can commit as followers of Christ is to do nothing. We can no longer go along to get along, with this generation. We have a responsibility to tell our youths that evil entertainment can harm them, whether they believe it or not. No one would stand for an entertainer wearing a Nazi uniform or a KKK outfit, so we shouldn't stand idly by while entertainers praise and promote evil and the prince of darkness."

Ben was thoughtful a moment, then slowly nodded. "All right, we'll call this a draw."

Dan laughed softly and leaned his head against his backpack as he put his earphones back on. "Now let me get back to my music. I've got some repair work to do."

Ben shook his head and smiled as he angled his body to lie down on the row of seats. "Dan," he said, loud enough to override the music, "make sure you donate that brain of yours to medical science when you die. They'll have a field day with that gray matter."

# CHAPTER FOURTEEN

## *The Evil Empire*

Patrolman Westin was feeling the strain of the long night shift as he poured himself another cup of strong coffee from his thermos. The steam from the hot java wafted up in the chilly patrol car and licked lazily at the cruiser's headliner. *Thank God for the diner.* Just as he started to take a sip, his cell phone rang.

"You're gonna owe me big-time for this one," quipped Gil Chandler breezily.

"Always do. How in the world do you sound so chipper at six in the morning? Are you still working, or did you get some sleep?"

"Couldn't get that kidnapping out of my mind, so I kept busy."

"Yeah, I'm the same way. I lost the damned pickup truck. Can't believe he got out of the area in this weather, with all the roads closed. What'd ya got?"

"Came up with a name for your truck driver. I ran some combinations of the plate number and got lucky."

"That's not luck, man, you're good."

"Yeah, I know, but I'm humble—now get ready to copy. That truck is registered to a Graeber Tank Lines, LLC, in Richmond, Virginia. Looks like it's what we thought it was, an owner-operator outfit. The only two officers of the company are a Fred Tanner and a Rob Williams, so I'm guessing one of them is your John Doe. I called their office and got voice mail. Don't expect to hear anything from them till later this morning. I'll let you know when they make contact."

"Thanks, man. You always come through. Now get some sleep. One of us needs to be able to think."

While waiting for the coffee to cool, Paul paused for a minute to reflect on his close friendship with Gil. As friends went, Gil was a good one. As a brother-in-law, he was great fun at ball games and family gatherings. Rather than turn bitter and withdrawn after the death of his wife, Paul's sister, Gil had become even more supportive and helpful to everyone in his life.

Paul realized how much he depended on Gil's help as he pulled back out on the slick road for one more try to find the elusive pickup. In another two hours, he'd be off the shift and have to leave it to the day crew. He didn't want to do that, though.

\*\*\*

In the now clammy and dimly lit terminal, a loud ring tone resonated through the gate area, startling Ben, who grabbed his phone to silence it. A few travelers nearby groaned at the loud intrusion and then nodded off back to sleep after shooting some pained expressions in Ben's direction. Ben mumbled to himself about the complexity of his phone as he fumbled to answer it.

"You did!" Ben exclaimed, and then cupped the phone in his hand to muffle his voice. "Good. Now go home; there's nothing more for you to do," Ben ordered with a firm tone. After pausing, he looked down and let out a deep breath.

"Everything all right?" Dan asked in a golf whisper.

"That was Adam calling. My office was still locked and completely intact when he got there. Hard to believe. Not a scratch anywhere. But five rooms down, part of a tree trunk was driven into the building like a giant javelin. What are the odds?"

"That's great news!" Dan said.

Ben remained silent as he stared at the floor.

Confused, Dan said, "If your office wasn't touched by the tornado, then you don't have to worry about your safe, right?"

"I'd rather not dwell on the safe right now. Haven't opened it in years."

Dan frowned. "I don't get it. Why were you so worried about a safe that you don't even open?"

Ben continued to look down. "Remember the grad assistant I had the affair with?" Ben asked quietly.

"Yeah."

"There's more to the story. She came back about six months after she left, and told me she was pregnant."

"Wow. That must have been a shocker. What'd you do?"

"The day she came into my office, I was dictating notes into my voice recorder. I put it down on the desk and left it recording while she talked. She wanted me to take responsibility for the baby—not marry her, but support her and the baby. I got her to admit she'd slept with her boyfriend after she broke off our affair. I got it all recorded."

Not good, Dan thought, and put on his investigator face. "Do you think it was your baby?"

Ben shrugged. "She said she'd done the math and was positive it was my child, but I wasn't so sure. Besides, she'd led me to believe she was on the pill, so I didn't feel responsible. Didn't matter, though. I didn't want anything to do with her or the baby then, and I was going to make sure she left me alone—permanently. Back then, paternity suits were real expensive, and I wasn't about to cooperate, so she was hoping to pressure me into supporting her."

"What about her boyfriend?"

"He dropped her as soon as he found out she was pregnant. She said she couldn't go to her parents because they were uptight socialites who'd never accept a grandchild born out of wedlock."

"So what'd she do?"

"After she finished talking, I held up the voice recorder and told her I'd gotten everything she'd said, and I made it clear I'd use the recording against her if she ever tried to pressure me. I also suggested there was another way of taking care of the problem. I gave her some money and showed her the door. Haven't seen her since and don't know what happened to her or if she had the baby."

Dan swallowed his anger. "Man, that's cold! Aren't you the least bit curious?"

"I keep the voice recorder locked in my safe in case she ever comes back. I've always told myself that I'll use her confession against her if she ever tries to sue me, but I don't know. I must be getting soft in my old age. I've actually caught myself wondering about the baby too, but I always come to my senses and stop that in a hurry."

*He's not a heartless monster, just a confused man with no compass.* Dan sighed. "You'll never stop thinking about that child. You know that, right?"

"Maybe so, but the damage is already done, so I guess you could say I have my own personal demons. If there is a hell, as you claim, I'm probably headed there. I'm certainly not proud of myself, especially over that."

Dan looked away and watched the people around him begin to stir in the cold building. "Everybody sins, Ben—it's how you handle it that makes the difference." He paused and turned toward Ben. "Now that you bring it up, how do rabbis handle the topic of hell?"

"I don't remember them ever mentioning it," Ben said.

"How about evil?"

"Yes, of course—they spoke about good and evil."

"How about evil spirits or demons?" prodded Dan.

"Can't say I recall ever hearing them mentioned in the synagogue, but why the fascination with the dark side? Just when you're starting to sound rational, you veer off into your fantasy world of the macabre."

"The existence of supernatural beings is clearly documented in the Bible. If you believe the Bible, you have to believe in the existence of demons and evil spirits. If they weren't important, Christ would have never mentioned them. Probably the most unique miracle Jesus ever performed time after time was the casting out of demons and evil spirits from people. No one had ever done that before his arrival on earth."

Ben shook his head. "You realize your quest to save souls is hopeless, don't you? You say you want to appeal to the average person with factual information, and then you start talking about ghouls and goblins. No one's gonna take you seriously."

Dan shook his head. "I want people to take the Bible seriously. The Bible describes Jesus casting out evil spirits and demons multiple times. The Book of Mark describes how Jesus cast out an evil spirit that his disciples had been unable to drive out. Christ actually said it was a particular kind of spirit that could only be driven out by prayer and fasting. I'd like to know more about them and where they are now. Do they have an impact on people today? If so, what can we do about it? We can't see them any more than we can see our spirit and soul, but the Bible is crystal clear in declaring they exist and warning us that they've declared war on us."

Ben barked a raspy laugh. "You should drop the subject and stick with your history lessons. If people want to learn about demons, all they have to do is go to the movies. Hollywood's done your work for you. You'll get a lot more people to listen to you if you forget the horror movie nonsense."

"I think the subject's important because some believe demons and evil spirits affect many people in their daily lives—in a bad way. I'm not just talking about full-blown possessions, like Linda Blair in *The Exorcist*, which are rare—at least in the U.S., but the evil oppression they inflict on everyday people through their unseen influence. People need to be made aware of the threat."

"I thought that was the church's job."

"It is," Dan replied. "Some say one of the main reasons Christ created the church in the first place was to fight evil—namely Satan's occupying force on earth. But many churches don't address the subject to any great extent. They're afraid they'll be labeled as lunatics."

"Doesn't the Catholic Church teach their priests how to conduct exorcisms?"

"They do - at least they used to. And they're not the only ones. A relatively new element - deliverance ministries - has sprung up to specifically address the impact of demons and evil spirits on people. It's a small part of the overall Christian Church. Christ was the first deliverance minister, so to speak. The current wave of deliverance ministries started in the 1970s. The more I've studied the subject, the more I realized how little the Church, as a whole, knows about the spiritual world. From what I've read, I've come to believe there are significant differences in the ways spirits and demons can affect people. Christ's own admission that different types of evil entities require different methods to drive them out is an indication that there is some complexity to the demonic world. Christians should be armed with some basic knowledge of demons and evil spirits to successfully defend themselves and others."

"What's the difference between a demon and an evil spirit?"

"Demons seem to be more powerful spiritual entities; certain types can actually possess a person. Evil spirits are lesser beings. Some are attracted to people whose souls are spiritually injured or to people who commit sinful or self-destructive acts, like taking drugs. A growing number of Christian researchers believe there is a wide variety of fallen immortal beings. They come in a lot of shapes and sizes and have different strengths and capabilities."

Ben asked, "If you believe no one in the Church understands the spirit world and the so-called demons inhabiting it, why worry about a problem that's not clearly defined?"

Dan groaned. "I believe what's stated in the Bible— demons and evil spirits exist—and Christ ordered his followers to cast them out in his name. As far as I can tell, his command has never been rescinded. Look at all the evil around the world. Haven't you ever wondered where it comes from?"

"It comes from man," Ben said, sweeping his arm in a wide arc. "We're perfectly capable of doing just about anything evil you can think of. Look what the Nazis did to my people during the Holocaust. Man doesn't need any help from things that go bump in the night in order to be evil."

"That's what I used to think too. I agree that some evil does come directly from fallen humans who were born with a propensity to sin, but I also think some of the more heinous crimes, like the Holocaust and the recent beheadings and crucifixions of Christians by Islamic terrorists, are inspired by evil spiritual beings. Once I started to read some of the exceptional NDE stories and compared their testimonies to what's in the Bible, I realized that demons may be hard at work behind the scenes right now, and we ignore it. Which, of course, is what they want."

"And exactly how does one avoid catching a demon or two? Wear demon repellent?" Ben snickered.

"Don't sin," Dan said in a serious tone. "Don't give them an opportunity to target you—and that includes being involved in anything related to the occult. If you were somehow introduced to satanic activity, say, as a child, or if you were victimized in a way that leaves you vulnerable to demonic attack—say, the victim of child abuse—then you would need someone with spiritual knowledge and experience to help you. For most of us, though, when we sin—and we all do—if we say prayers that directly address our sinful acts and our desire to break free from any demonic influence in our life, that's about it. Invoke the name of Jesus Christ and be sincere."

"That's it?"

"That would eliminate some demonic harassment, if you keep at it," Dan replied. "Demons may tempt you, but if you resist, they ultimately give up. Some think the Bible's instructions are complex, but many are pretty straightforward. I think the Bible also teaches us that Jesus Christ's battles against particular demons were purely defensive. He intervened only when specific individuals were under attack or control—he didn't go on the offensive against the entire demonic hierarchy. He obviously had a reason for not doing so, and we should take heed of his actions. He also taught us that we must use his spiritual power and the Holy Spirit to ward off or cast out demons—not our own power, which we really don't have."

"You're back to your invisible world where you don't have a shred of proof that any of these beings exist!" Ben said, a little too loudly.

Enjoying Ben's interest, Dan replied, "They exist, but not in our dimension where we can see or sense them except on rare occasions. I think we've seen some recent eyewitness accounts that point to the temporary appearance of evil entities in our physical plane. Not too long ago, a woman in Gary, Indiana, claimed her seven-year-old son was possessed. It made the evening news across the country. Police went out to investigate, then a social worker, and finally a priest. What got everyone's attention was that a nurse and a social worker witnessed the boy walking up a wall backward in the hospital's emergency room. He had to be restrained by five grown men. It's all documented in news reports."

"Nothing but tabloid nonsense," Ben said, waving a hand.

"Google it and see for yourself. There was another case in July 2014 where a TV news team went to a home in Hanover, Pennsylvania, to investigate claims by a family that they were being harassed by evil spirits. When the reporter and the camera operator entered the house, the cameraman was scratched on the wrist by an invisible entity. They showed the abrasion right after it happened. The reporter also claimed she was touched and pinched. The entire segment was shown on a local TV news program. You can see the video online and judge for yourself."

"Anyone can manipulate video to create false stories."

"True," Dan said, "but I don't think they're fabrications. People dismiss what they don't understand. Hospital psych wards are full of people who hear voices telling them to do evil things. Some of them have physical malfunctions of the brain, no doubt, but I suspect some are under demonic attack. Now that we have instant news 24/7, we're hearing about this more and more. We also have a lot of video camera footage from around the world showing unexplained anomalies that could be either demonic or angelic. I know that man is fallen and has a sinful nature; however, I think we're getting more than a little help from the demonic world."

"A little help from our demonic friends, huh?" Ben said. "Let's face it, man is plain evil. We don't need any little green goblins to tempt us to do bad things; we do them because we want to—they feel good and bring us pleasure. We're animals, like every other creature on earth."

Dan raised his hands in the air and sighed loudly. "We're not. God created only man with a conscience and the ability to think and pray in the abstract. The body through the spirit and soul is the connection point of attack for demons, and they do it in an organized, systematic way."

Ben asked, "Organized?"

"NDE witnesses who claim to have entered the supernatural realm report that demons are sent to earth to tempt, oppress, and yes, in some cases, possess specific human beings—preselected targets. It's not a random process where demons float around and yell 'Boo' in the dark. The Bible makes reference to the potentially staggering large numbers of demons in existence. Their primary goal is to influence man to commit sin and continue sinning. I think they also plant false ideas to confuse and mislead people. Many researchers believe that demons are active intermittently in our physical dimension in others way too, and they're poised to take direct action on earth near the end times."

"And how do they convince people to sin?"

"No one knows the exact mechanism they use, and the Bible doesn't give a description. Some writers on the subject claim demons are able to project thoughts and urges from their supernatural realm into the minds of their human targets. They can be as simple as negative thoughts about a person or an event, or more specific and pernicious, as urges to hurt or kill someone. One NDE witness described the inter-dimensional demonic communication system as their emitting low-frequency tones in the form of musical notes that somehow strike the target's spirit and soul. The bottom line is they somehow can meld their suggestive thoughts into the victim's stream of consciousness and make it appear that the victim was the source of the thoughts. Imagine a demon pumping negative thoughts about a spouse into a victim's mind. The end result could be divorce. Worse, if the demon keeps projecting thoughts about abusing a child or going on a shooting rampage, and the victim doesn't recognize the source of the thoughts—the results could be tragic."

"So they whisper in your ear to be bad? Is that it? Like Flip Wilson used to say, 'The devil made me do it'?"

"That's a crude analogy, but yes, Ben. I think it may be true, but probably much more sophisticated and complex than how I described it. The key is to analyze your thoughts and stop negative ones that pop into your head. Man has an imagination and the ability to create thoughts. If you sense that negative urges have popped into your mind out of nowhere, then it might be a demonic projection. The answer is to rebuke Satan and his demons, out loud, in the name of Jesus Christ, and the thoughts will most likely stop."

"Dan, do you have any idea how ridiculous you sound? You're suggesting we should walk around shouting, 'Demons, out,'—based on the belief that there's some army of evil spirits that skulks around and puts nasty thoughts in your head."

"Yeah, I know it sounds nuts, but that's about right. Keep an open mind. You can't dismiss out of hand the NDE witnesses who report observing activity that tracks with the Scriptures. What was the spiritual warfare the Apostle Paul talked about? If we don't see any battles going on around us, then they must be happening somewhere else. I believe it happens in the spiritual realm, where our spirits serve as a connection point for our minds and souls. The Bible tells us that when Satan and his minions are banished from earth for a thousand years after Christ's return, we'll have peace on earth. Why? Because we won't have evil entities who tempt and deceive us and create havoc. In their place, we'll have the incomparable love of Jesus Christ. Until that day, we'll have to be on guard and use the defenses the Bible teaches us."

Ben said, "And why isn't any of this taught as a subject in college? If there are these hordes of demons in some hierarchy, as you claim, why don't the clergy produce an order of battle that's disseminated to the hallowed ranks of the faithful? Every combat force needs a strategy."

"I could speculate, but I don't know. Like NDEs and OBEs, I don't think most major Christian denominations spend any time studying the subject. There are some prominent pastors who do give excellent sermons on the topic of Satan, and a number of researchers have written excellent books on the subject. Most of the secular colleges and universities which have parapsychology and spirituality courses are in Europe, but Bible-based instruction about the spiritual world of evil beings is done on an ad hoc basis by a relatively small number of Christian teachers."

"You're on shaky ground, Dan, if even the majority of your hallowed pastors don't talk about the subject. I have to admit, though, your inclination to do more research on the topic is logical. Self-study is important when tackling a subject matter ignored by the establishment."

Dan laughed and tapped Ben on the arm. "We agree on that, anyway. I find the topic interesting and I keep learning more all the time. I'll give you an example. At least two NDE witnesses have concluded, based on their experiences, that demons also are responsible for some human illnesses. They independently corroborate what's in the Bible."

"Illnesses? Mental or physical?"

"Both. Where do you think polio, Ebola, and AIDS came from?"

"Where every other disease comes from. Bacteria and viruses, and they resulted from cellular mutations in the bodies of organisms, including humans."

"Why the mutations? Did you ever wonder how they started? I don't know and neither do you. I think it's an interesting concept, and when compared to the Bible, it holds up. In the Book of Luke in the New Testament, Christ made a specific reference to a spirit that had caused a woman to be crippled. After he healed her by expelling the spirit, he stated that Satan had kept her bound for eighteen years. To me, that's evidence that evil spirits can cause physical ailments in people."

"So, according to your beliefs, people are wasting their time going to doctors."

"Not at all. The Book of Luke has a number of passages specifically describing how Jesus went into crowds and healed some of their physical maladies and some from conditions caused by evil spirits. The body does break down and many of the illnesses and diseases we get are not caused by demons. But I suspect *some* medical conditions we believe are purely physical may have a spiritual source, only most ignore the possibility that prayer might heal them.

"Many people interpret the results of Christ's crucifixion and resurrection to have included not only a cleansing of the sins of believers, but also the cleansing of the physical bodies of believers who pray for healing. We have to learn how to unleash the power of the Holy Spirit within us and cause it to flow from our spirit, through our soul, into our physical bodies. To do that, you must have strong faith. I think it's a basic concept anyone can understand."

Ben grimaced. "Okay, but that doesn't track with a loving God, does it? Why would a one-year-old die of cancer? He can't pray his way to healing at the age of one, can he?"

"That's the only concept which really confused me at first. Why God would allow Satan or demons to attack certain people even though they didn't commit a particular sin—like a child or a Christian who tries very hard not to sin."

"Exactly! How can you claim to have a God of love if he allows demons to torment people, and, for that matter, why did your all-loving God even create demons in the first place?"

"Legitimate questions. I asked the same ones myself. My understanding of the Bible is that God created the spiritual beings that are demons today, but he didn't make them demons—he created them as angels. Sounds crazy, but that's what the Bible says. They corrupted themselves when they rebelled with Satan, and God expelled them from heaven and sent them to the heavenly abode that intersects with earth. The demons exercised their wills when they made the conscious decision to disobey God."

"Angels turned into demons? How's that possible?" Ben asked.

"We don't know the process, but we do know the result. The Bible states that God threw one third of the angels out of heaven with Satan. Since angels are immortal beings, they continue to exist, but since they have been cut off from the loving energy of God, they somehow morphed into demons." Dan lifted both hands in front of himself, saying, "I know it sounds bizarre, but if you dig through the Bible, you'll find a number of passages that describe what we would call science fiction."

"Let's say I accept your theory that the expelled angels became demons. That still doesn't explain how a good God would allow them to torment creations he supposedly loves."

"Ben, I think the confusion comes from humans inserting the word 'allow' into conversations about God. In the vast majority of cases, it's not a question of God allowing anything; it's a matter of man suffering the consequences of his own sin or the sin of others. Beyond that, the key point to remember is that Satan and his evil horde are the ones administering the torment, not God. God doesn't want it, and he's given us tools in the Bible to fight it. I also believe there's a difference between punishment and discipline. God won't intervene if we decide to sin, but he will provide us an opportunity to use the consequences of our sin as a learning tool and an opportunity to grow, spiritually. The net result is the discipline we receive from suffering the consequences of our sin; it allows us to learn important lessons that help us later in life."

"All right, but why does God allow demons to harass people?"

"Again, *allow* is not the right term. God turned over authority of earth to Adam and Eve, and they gave it to Satan when they sinned. Christ gave us back the authority over Satan and his demons when he died on the cross, but we must use the power that God describes in the Bible. If we don't, Satan and his demons will continue to harass us if we let them. We're stuck with the current order until Christ returns.

"Based on what I've read, if you consciously decide to sin, you attract demons who further tempt and influence you. Some believe our penalty for sin on earth is that we get to have demons stay with us and bring the misery they inflict. The Bible even states that if we get rid of a demon but don't fill our souls with the Holy Spirit, the old demon will return with seven of his buddies."

"That might explain my mood swings," Ben said, and laughed.

Ignoring the joke, Dan said, "Since demons do exist and have the ability to operate on earth for the time being, they function as a form of discipline and as a de facto control mechanism. If demons couldn't touch us, there wouldn't be any penalty at all for sin while we're on earth. Demons are a control mechanism as well as a form of earthly discipline. God doesn't direct them to do evil; they make the decision that is part of their nature. God helps us learn from our mistakes. The more we know about demons and evil spirits, the better prepared we are to recognize their presence and resist them. We'd also be a lot more conscious of the results of sin."

"You seem fixated on the notion of sin."

Dan shifted in his seat and stretched out his legs. He gave Ben a small smile. He was on comfortable ground now.

"I am. Whether we like it or not, the Bible makes clear that God will judge us for the sins we commit while on earth if we're not born again. Some theologians and Christian laypeople give the impression that once we're saved from judgment by God's grace through faith, we don't have to worry about sinning anymore. The truth is, if we, as Christians, sin, we reap the consequences by having demon companions who make us miserable. Not to mention we disappoint God, which separates us from him. Once you really believe, you don't want to do that."

"Most people get pleasure out of sinful acts, so how are demons a deterrent?"

"If you sin on a constant basis and have no faith, some believe the demons leave you alone and allow you to sin yourself into hell. On the other hand, people who have had their moment of true belief develop a much keener conscience, so any type of sin bothers them."

"You still haven't explained how your God can be just if he allows demons to exist."

"I think demons are a form of discipline you receive for not following God's commands, like most loving parents discipline their children if they misbehave. Although God doesn't want demons to torment us, he will use the actions of demons as a test to see if we're sincere in our faith. As Christians, if we claim to have had an MTB, yet secretly desire to keep sinning, God knows we're not heaven material."

"What about the demons in hell that you claim exist? How is their eternal torment of so-called lost souls the result of a loving God? People in hell have already been tested and failed, according to what you're saying."

"God is unconditionally loving and uncompromisingly just. He has warned us in the Bible and through teachers that we will reap what we sow. If you don't repent and accept Christ during your physical life, you'll get what God promised in your spiritual life—judgment and punishment for your sins. A promise is a promise. My advice is to take the Bible seriously. From what I've gathered from some of the extensive NDE and OBE witnesses who have gone to hell, you'll get back all of the negative you gave out in life."

"Why doesn't your God end everything now and spare us all the misery?"

"No idea. The Bible says God has his own timetable for everything—and when he acts, everything he planned will have been completed."

"You still dodged a major question. What about the bad things that happen to good people?"

"Since we live in a fallen world, some of us will suffer from undeserved tragedies that are not caused by God, but by Satan and his evil empire. A burglar doesn't care if you're a good person when he breaks into your house and steals your valuables, and Satan and his hordes could care less if you're a small child or a kind Christian—you're fair game. A temporary broken world produces brokenness in people's lives, even untimely death. We have to accept it because we can't change it. And, we keep faith that God is with us through those times if we call on him. The Bible warns us that we will face sorrows during our physical lives. I know it doesn't make any sense to us at the time of the hardship, but in the end it can be used for our benefit if we call on God's power. The discomfort we suffer in this very short lifetime is nothing compared to the joy we'll experience in heaven."

Ben jabbed at his new friend by saying, "You're still dodging."

Dan shook his head. "No, I'm not, but it's not easy stuff to explain. Here's a basic analogy. Let's say a deer runs out into the middle of the road and gets hit by a car. The deer was trying to get across the road, and the driver of the car didn't have enough time to stop. Neither had evil intent, but the deer ends up in agony, with life-threatening injuries. The driver stops the car and calls a veterinarian friend to come to the scene. The deer is in shock and in great pain, and when the vet tries to give the animal a shot of pain-killer before moving him, the deer goes berserk. First, the animal is struck by the huge machine, the car; and now this strange-looking creature, the vet, is trying to stick a sharp needle into the deer which initially will make it suffer more. In many respects, the innocent human is like the deer. We don't recognize actions by God that are meant to help—all we know is that they are painful at the time."

"Yeah, I get it," Ben said, "but if God protected you as if he loved you, he could spare you all the pain and still come up with a plan that doesn't involve suffering for the innocent."

"Like I said, Christ made it clear that we would face trials and suffering while on earth. God uses it as part of his preparation for us to function in heaven. You know, it's funny we celebrate the sacrifices and suffering that a great athlete endures, but when God uses a painful event in our lives for our own good, we curse him."

"And we should, Dan. There's way too much suffering in this world to give God any credit for having a good life."

"Look at you. You get paid a nice salary to read books and give lectures in historic buildings. Not exactly the hard life. I'm in the same category. I've had way more pleasure than pain in my life, and a lot of the pain I did suffer was self-inflicted. I know most people don't have what we consider to be a blessed life, but in actuality, the ones who have it harder actually have it easier in some respects. They don't have any distractions from wealth to get in the way of their faith. Sounds nuts, but the rich may have a harder time being faithful to God than the poor because of all their worldly distractions."

With a tired smile, Ben said, "I think I'll stick to my delayed entry program and have as much fun as I can. If you're smart, you'll do the same."

# CHAPTER FIFTEEN

## *The Rubber Meets the Road*

"Richie," Joy cried from her cocoon of jackets in the front seat of the pickup, "something's wrong. Oh God, something's wrong. I've got so much pain, Richie—"

He shook the sleep from his head and tried to focus on her. "Where's the pain? What kind of pain?"

"Oh my God, I don't know. Horrible pain. It's got to be the baby. Please do something …."

He straightened himself behind the steering wheel and braced his shaking hands. "I'll get you help, I promise. Just hold on, okay? I'll get you to the hospital. They'll know what to do, but you gotta hold on."

\*\*\*

"Gotcha!"

Patrolman Westin watched from his hiding place behind a stand of trees as the red pickup streaked past him. He'd been making the rounds of the major roads in hopes of catching a glimpse of the truck and had decided to set up on a main road.

He pulled out of his favorite spot, normally used for running radar, and lagged behind the truck by about a hundred yards. He could barely make out the plate in front of him, but as he got closer, he was able to read X75. Paul radioed in for backup and announced he was in pursuit of a kidnapping suspect who might be armed and dangerous. He increased his speed and engaged his lights and siren. The chase was heading away from the Douglas-Charlotte Airport.

\*\*\*

Although dawn was less than an hour away, the heavy cloud cover kept the area blanketed in darkness. The normally strong glow of the airport's outside lights into the night sky was missing.

On alert for the intermittent blackouts, Ben nervously gripped Dan's trusty flashlight—ready to click it on the moment darkness in turn hit the terminal. *What would I have done if this man hadn't sat here? What if he'd been someone who wouldn't talk to me about all this craziness? I'd have lost my mind in the darkness.* He didn't want to sleep, and talking with Dan helped … though the poor man was probably well past exhaustion from his trip and their long, long night. A night soon to be over.

"You know, I finally figured out what your problem is," Ben blurted out, disrupting Dan's light sleep. "You're not living in the present; you're focused on some imaginary future."

Dan snapped awake and faced Ben with bleary eyes. "I thought you were asleep."

"I can't sleep. I don't understand. You put your life on hold just to believe in some invisible God—and for what? To get fire insurance? What kind of life is that?" Ben demanded.

"My life's not on hold. Every day has meaning and a reason for getting up in the morning. And right now, you're my reason. It's not fire insurance, it's life forever—in this body and in the next one—with someone who loves me more than I could ever imagine."

"But your focus is on some invisible entity. That's what your life's all about—convincing yourself every day to believe in something you can't see, so you don't lose your precious faith."

"Ben, the main point of a Christian's existence is not solely to believe in God. Our goal is to give love to everyone in every way we can, as God loves us. The small sacrifices we make on earth to serve God are more than rewarded in heaven."

"Ha! You made my point. You admitted that Christians must live a life of sacrifice and resist pleasures. What kind of life is that?"

"Christians get pleasure out of everyday life, like everyone else, but we also get great satisfaction from loving others, serving them, and convincing nonbelievers there is an unseen reality all around them. That's pleasure on a real-time basis—the psychological rewards of faith. I could go through life believing in God on an intellectual level only, but it would be empty and meaningless if I didn't practice my faith through action. A Christian doesn't focus on himself, or herself—they focus on others. Most importantly, they focus on spreading the truth about Jesus Christ."

Dan was like no other man Ben had ever met. *What would life actually be like without fear of losing everything you've worked for?* "You actually believe this, don't you?" he asked.

"Yeah, I do. When I had my moment of true belief, my MTB, everything inside me changed—literally. My spiritual wiring became brand-new. It's instinct now, and really, you have the same instincts buried under layers of scar tissue and corrosion in your soul. You can't access it because you've allowed yourself to become hardened and blinded to what is all around you and in you."

"I live in the present, Dan. I seek the truth too, but don't believe in living a life of wishful thinking."

"You know, I bet your soul still has some light left in it even though you don't believe it. I'll bet if you saw a bridge collapse and then saw a car full of people speeding toward it, you'd do everything in your power to stop them."

"I guess I would, but anyone would," Ben murmured. *I would, wouldn't I?*

"Not really. Some are so hardened, they don't care about anyone but themselves. Some have even allowed evil to overwhelm them, and they'd get pleasure from watching the car plunge off the bridge."

"I suppose that's true, but I don't see how you'll ever get people to *have* an MTB, as you call it. I think you're wasting your time." Ben looked down at his watch. "We've been talking now, off and on, for hours. I'll grant you have a unique perspective, but here I am and nothing's changed."

Dan laughed. "Keep in mind that I can't change your spirit and soul or cause a moment of true belief—only God can. I can lay out the most compelling case possible about the existence of God and Jesus Christ, but only God can convict your heart and renew your spirit—no human can. But you can start the process by accepting the inner call of Christ. It may all sound like a bunch of gobbledygook, but the process is as real as that seat you're sitting on."

Ben covered his mouth and began coughing uncontrollably. *Oh God, not now ....* "I've got more important things to worry about," he said, his voice raspy as he tried to catch his breath. He grasped at his shirt collar with one hand and gasped to gain air.

Out came the inhaler. Ben made two quick squirts and inhaled deeply.

Dan observed him carefully, obviously concerned. "Are you all right, Ben?"

"Yeah, yeah." Ben waved his hands, though it took all his energy to do it. He swallowed hard and looked up at Dan. "Maybe I need food. Do you want to look for a place that's open for breakfast?"

"I can definitely use something to eat," Dan said, getting to his feet. "Are you sure you're okay? You look awfully pale. I can go get us something and bring it back if you want to stay here and rest." He adjusted the backpack onto his shoulders.

Ben shook his head. He'd been here before and knew he'd survive this attack, too. "Maybe we can find someplace close by."

Dan picked up Ben's briefcase while Ben struggled to get to his feet.

"Let's go," Ben ordered unconvincingly.

They moved slowly through the concourse, looking for an open coffee shop or snack bar. Ben's gait was unsteady, but somehow he was able to keep pace with Dan.

Seeing a coffee shop open nearby brought a rush of relief. *Thank you, Lord*, Dan thought without reservation.

He turned to Ben and asked, "How about some coffee and a muffin?"

"Sounds good to me."

Ben and Dan each ordered their coffee and pastry and made their way to a nearby table and chairs. After sipping a latte and biting into a big bran muffin, Dan gazed out into the terminal, and without facing Ben, started to talk as if on autopilot.

Ben was relieved he didn't have to make conversation now. *This attack seems different, somehow.*

Dan said, "I have to be honest. When you first sat next to me and we starting talking, I thought our conversation wouldn't last ten minutes. I never thought I'd be able to debate a liberal academic, and truthfully, I've never wanted to. But now that we've talked, I not only have a clearer understanding of my own beliefs, I also have a better appreciation of your legitimate questions about faith."

"And maybe you'll eventually see the light," Ben said with a slight chuckle.

Dan swallowed a bit of muffin and smiled. "I don't think our meeting was an accident. Whatever the outcome, I think we'll both be better for tonight."

A stab of pain in Ben's left arm was excruciating. It radiated through his back and took away what little breath he had left.

"Ben! What is it?"

"My arm …. "He began to shake uncontrollably as an ice-cold sweat covered his body.

Dan grabbed him by his shoulders to prevent him from falling forward. Then he lifted Ben out of his seat and guided him onto the floor.

Ben moaned while lying on his back. "Dan …."

"Hang on—I'm going to get you some help."

Dan looked down at the crumpled figure on the floor. Still grabbing his left arm, Ben had pulled himself into a near-fetal position. Dan could see his chest continue to rise and fall.

*Good. At least he's breathing*, Dan thought. He touched Ben's carotid artery and could feel a weak pulse.

By now, several people in the concourse had run over to them.

"What's wrong?" shouted a woman.

"My friend needs a doctor—please get us some help."

The woman rushed away as several other people began to crowd around them.

"Ben, I'm going to get help. Hold on."

Unable to talk, Ben grimaced with his eyes tightly shut.

Dan thought of what he could do. He looked up at the man leaning closest to him. "We need some aspirin!"

The man looked surprised as he straightened and then disappeared from view.

Dan could hear an announcement over the loudspeaker: "A physician is needed in Concourse C. If any medical personnel are available, medical assistance is needed in Concourse C."

A growing crowd had gathered around Dan and Ben. Completely ashen, Ben lay on the floor with his head propped on someone's jacket. Just then, the young sailor Dan had met at the food court knelt next to the pair on the floor.

"Sir, I'll take it from here." He immediately pressed his fingers against Ben's neck, as Ben grimaced and continued to clutch his left arm.

"Man, am I glad to see you," Dan confided in a low voice. "My friend here collapsed while we were eating. I think he's having a heart attack."

"Yes, sir, I believe you're right. We need to get him to a hospital now. He still has a pulse, but it's very weak."

Dan grabbed his phone and dialed 911 while the corpsman attended to Ben.

A wiry older man pushed through the crowd and, kneeling next to Dan, Ben, and the corpsman, said, "I'm a doctor." He elbowed the corpsman out of the way and began to check for vital signs, oblivious to the corpsman's presence.

As the doctor checked Ben's pulse, three medics pulled up in a white Medic EMS club cart. Still apparently groggy from the early hour, the two men and the woman dressed in dark navy jackets sat motionless and stared at Ben lying on the floor.

The doctor shouted, "We have a medical emergency here! We need an ambulance and this man needs to get to a hospital!"

As if awakened from a trance, the EMS techs got off the cart and began to unstrap a stretcher.

"I just called 911. They're on their way," Dan announced.

Ben gasped as his eyes opened wide—then they shut and he seemed to go limp.

The doctor frantically felt for his pulse and put his ear over Ben's mouth.

"Does he have a pulse?" Dan asked rhetorically, dreading that Ben had died.

"This man's gone into cardiac arrest." The doctor quickly leaned over and began chest compressions.

Without thinking, Dan grabbed Ben's arm and began to pray quietly.

"Sir, do you mind? I'm trying to work here," the doctor shouted.

Startled and embarrassed, Dan pulled away. After calming himself, he fought to suppress a flash of anger welling inside him. Sensing he needed to act, Dan made sure he was out of the doctor's way and slowly reached for Ben's left ankle as the doctor continued chest compressions.

Dan prayed to himself a simple prayer of healing and mercy for Ben.

"Good grief, man, I asked you to stay out of the way. I'm trying to save this man's life!"

Ben stiffened and then relaxed while making a choking sound.

The doctor froze for a second and then reached for Ben's neck. "He has a pulse," he shouted.

Ben began writhing on the floor as more and more people circled around them and gawked at the spectacle.

Dan felt joy flood into him as Ben shook his head from side to side while his eyes were tightly shut. He seemed highly agitated. Dan let his temporary anger subside as a sense of relief began to sweep over him. *Agitation means he's fighting, right?*

Dan leaned down near Ben's ear and spoke in a hushed but forceful tone: "You're not going anywhere. You have a daughter waiting for you. I'm praying for you."

Out of his peripheral vision, Dan could see ambulance EMT personnel approaching at a fast pace. They quickly took control of the scene as the doctor and the corpsman stood and stepped back. By now the man had returned with a package of aspirin, but he stopped when he saw the medical personnel.

"This man's having a cardiac emergency; he needs to get to an emergency room," the doctor said for all to hear.

One of the EMT techs nodded and began rooting through a carrying case as another tech reached for a portable oxygen bottle.

While they transferred Ben to an ambulance stretcher, one of the techs asked if anyone was traveling with him.

"I am," Dan blurted out without hesitation. "We're traveling together."

"Okay, you can come with us to the hospital."

Dan followed. They wheeled Ben down to the terminal entrance and loaded his stretcher into a waiting ambulance. Though daybreak was technically fewer than thirty minutes away, dark clouds streaked with gray kept the early-morning air cloaked in darkness.

The road in front of the terminal doors looked freshly salted and scraped. The freezing rain had stopped and a thin layer of melting ice and salt remained on the road.

The slamming of the ambulance's front door jolted Dan's attention back to Ben. He climbed into the back of the ambulance with two of the EMT techs. "Can I ride back here with my friend?"

"Okay, but sit on that seat by the door."

The emergency techs swung the ambulance door shut with a thud, and Dan felt the acceleration as they pulled away from the terminal. Ben was now attached to a vital signs unit. A tech placed an oxygen mask over Ben's ashen face. He lay motionless on the stretcher while the techs worked calmly around him, inserting IVs and attaching monitor leads.

"Sir, what's the patient's name?" one tech asked, hunched over a laptop.

"Ben Chernick," Dan said, slipping off his backpack.

"Are you a relative?"

"No, an acquaintance. I mean, a friend. We're headed to Jacksonville together." Dan realized he was clutching Ben's briefcase like a lifeline.

"Do you know his next of kin?"

"He has a daughter in Florida. Her name is Ruth. He was going to visit her."

Dan opened Ben's briefcase and probed through the jumbled contents. A yellow piece of paper protruding out of a paperback caught Dan's eye. He pulled it out and saw the words: Ruth Williams, 117 Pelican Road, Palm Coast, followed by a phone number.

Dan read out her name and address.

"Will someone be contacting her?"

Dan said, "Yes, I—"

The loud, steady tone of the vitals monitor cut off Dan's statement. Dan could see clearly that one of the monitor lines had gone flat and another one nearly flat.

"He's in asystole!"

One of the techs opened Ben's shirt and the other began chest compressions. After a series of compressions that seemed to last an eternity, Ben's heart began to beat, but it was wildly erratic.

"Clear!" the tech called.

Ben's body arched upward as the voltage from the defibrillator paddles coursed through him. The jumbled tone of the monitor seemed to grow louder as Ben's heart raced out of control.

"Clear!" The tech administered a second surge of current. Ben's body again arched upward. The lines remained erratic.

"We're losing him. Clear!"

The tech administered a third surge of current into Ben's now almost lifeless body. No response ... then the steady tone of a flatline. Quickly the techs switched positions and began CPR.

Dan felt a sense of hopelessness as he looked at Ben lying like a mannequin; his body lurched each time one of the techs performed a chest compression.

*Pray!* The word distinctly rang out in Dan's mind as if someone was conversing with him.

Dan reached to touch Ben's leg and bowed his head. In the midst of his prayer, he looked up for a second at the techs. One of them nodded.

"Father God, please spare Ben's life. Please have mercy on him and restore him." Dan continued aloud as the techs performed the chest compressions.

Dan felt the ambulance speed up and heard the warble of the siren.

He continued praying. After what seemed an interminable amount of time, the loud, steady tone of the monitor stopped for a second and then resumed with soft regular beeps.

"He's back!"

Ben lurched up and began writhing. His eyes were wide open with a look of terror, and he was making anguished groans into the oxygen mask.

The techs worked to restrain him. "Sir, please try to relax!"

Ben continued to shake his head violently and struggle with the techs.

"Sir, you'll be all right, please relax!" One of the techs inserted a syringe into Ben's IV line and squeezed in a clear liquid.

Ben began to calm down just as the ambulance came to a stop in front of the hospital's emergency room. As the back door swung open, Dan felt the rush of cold morning air flood in. For the first time in hours, he realized he hadn't slept in two days.

A team of hospital emergency room staff off-loaded Ben and the stretcher and raced toward the emergency room doors. The melting ice sloshed beneath their feet as they trotted in near unison through the hospital entrance. Dan nearly slipped and lost his balance when his shoes lost traction in the icy slush. The hospital staff quickly wheeled Ben into a treatment room as Dan ran to keep up while clutching Ben's briefcase and his backpack.

The flight! Dan suddenly remembered their 7:00 a.m. flight to Jacksonville. He caught a glimpse of the time on a large wall clock and realized he wasn't going to make it, but at that point his sole focus was on Ben, his new friend who needed him. Ben was a grizzled old contrarian, but underneath his rough exterior, Dan knew he was a good man who'd gone astray. *Or maybe he'd simply never even known the way.*

A team of nurses, EMT techs, and doctors hovered over Ben as they lifted his limp body onto a hospital bed. Dan stood to one side of the room's entrance and watched with a mixture of relief and alarm as they began reattaching monitor patches and IV lines.

A young nurse looked at Dan with obvious concern and compassion on her face. "Sir, you can go to the waiting area. We'll come and get you when your friend is stabilized."

Dan walked into the adjoining waiting area and collapsed in a chair. The time was 6:45 a.m. Dan pulled out his cell phone and dialed the number for Ben's daughter.

"Hello, Mrs. Williams?" Dan asked the sleepy voice on the other end of the line.

"Yes?"

"My name is Dan Lucas. I'm traveling on a flight with your father, Ben Chernick. I'm calling from the Mercy Medical Center in Charlotte, North Carolina."

"My father? You're calling from a Charlotte hospital?"

"Yes, ma'am. Your father is traveling to see you, and while we were waiting for a flight to Jacksonville, he suffered a heart attack in the airport. He's been brought to the hospital. I don't know what his condition is, but he appears to have stabilized for now."

There was a long silence on the phone. "Oh my God! Is he all right?"

"I haven't heard from the doctors yet, but he's still alive. He's in the emergency room now; they've started working on him. I'll let you know as soon as I know something."

Ruth remained silent for another long pause. Then: "I'm going to book a flight right now. I'll call you back as soon as I have reservations. Call right away if there's any change!"

"Yes, ma'am, I will. Ma'am?" Dan heard the plea in his voice and didn't care.

"Please call me Ruth," she said.

"Ruth, your father is a good man and he really cares about you. This trip is important to him. I think he's going to be all right, but please pray for him."

"I will. Thank you."

Dan put away his phone and rubbed his weary eyes.

Just then, a group of EMT techs and a nurse wheeled Ben's bed out of the triage area, heading toward large double doors.

Dan ran over to the bed. Ben's eyes were closed and his face was gray as wet cement. He had an oxygen mask on and was attached to several IV lines, plus a monitor traveled with him.

"Where are you taking him?" Dan asked.

"ICU. Are you family?"

"I'm a friend; we're traveling together. His daughter's on the way."

"He's being admitted. Will you hold his valuables?"

"Yes."

The nurse handed Dan a plastic bag with Ben's wallet, watch, and keys. As the gurney was about to go through the doors, one of the nurses turned toward Dan. "You can get to ICU through the corridor off the main waiting area. You should get an update soon. This man's not going anywhere."

"Is he going to make it?" Dan asked, almost afraid of the answer.

"You'll need to talk to the doctor," she replied before disappearing with the rest of the medical entourage.

Dan felt anything but peaceful as he made his way to the waiting area. He sat in the closest chair, and then Connie came to mind. He quickly placed a call.

"Hon, I'm in a Charlotte hospital."

"What?" she nearly shouted.

"Shhh, I'm fine. A man on my flight had a heart attack and I came to the hospital with him."

"You did what?"

Dan sighed. He had absolutely no energy left. "Look, it's a long story. I'll explain when I get home. Right now I'm waiting for the man's daughter to fly in from Palm Coast. Once she gets here, I'll get a flight and come straight home."

"Sienna and Phil are at the hospital, you know."

"What time did they get there?"

"About five this morning. Phil called. Sienna has more than a UTI; she has an infection of the placenta lining and the hospital wants to induce. The baby's heartbeat is elevated, so they want to deliver as soon as possible. I know you wanted to be here, but the baby may be here before you get home."

"I'll start working on a flight right now and leave as soon as Ben's daughter gets here. This man's on his deathbed, and I don't want to go without someone being here."

"Dan, you're a good man. But don't forget your daughter. This is your first granddaughter. I love you."

"Love you too."

Dan felt the guilt rush back. He had to keep his promise to Sienna. One way or another, he had to return before the baby was born.

Dan found his way to the information desk in the main lobby. His adrenaline rush that kicked in when Ben had his heart attack was starting to subside, and Dan was now starting to feel complete exhaustion.

A cheerful elderly woman directed him to the visitor entrance of the ICU. She said, "My, you made it through the storm. You're one of the lucky ones!"

"I guess you could say that. I came from the airport; my friend was admitted."

"I'm sorry to hear that. Regular visiting hours are unlimited, but ICU is closed for visitation from 6:00 to 8:00 p.m."

Dan's phone rang.

"This is Ruth Williams, Mr. Lucas. How's my dad?"

"He's in ICU now. That's where I'm headed. They admitted him, so I don't have an update."

"I see. Thank you. I have a ten forty-five flight out of Jacksonville that's scheduled to arrive at Charlotte at twelve oh nine. I should be at the hospital by around 1:00 p.m. What's the address again?"

Dan looked around for some information and found a hospital brochure on a shelf.

"We're at the Carolinas Medical Center-Mercy, 2001 Vail Avenue. I'd say we're about five or ten miles from the airport."

"Okay. Thank you so much for staying with my father. I'll call you before my flight leaves Jacksonville."

"That's fine, Ruth. I'm glad I was able to be here with your father. I'll keep praying for him."

"Thank you again. I'll see you soon."

Dan wound his way among the hallways to the ICU and found Ben's room. Two nurses tended to Ben as he lay on a thick hospital bed surrounded by a console filled with monitoring equipment.

Ben's body was motionless. Dan walked over and looked down at Ben's ashen face. Ben's breathing was shallow and labored under the oxygen mask.

Dan said to him, "I thought we lost you, but you're too stubborn to check out early."

Ben looked up at Dan and then closed his eyes and rolled his head to the side. The oxygen mask prevented him from talking.

"We still have a lot to talk about," Dan stated, "and this little episode isn't going to stop me."

Ben did not respond. Dan patted him on the shoulder.

A nurse walked in and advised that Ben was being taken to the cath lab for a cardiac catheterization to check for blockage.

"Let's go find out what's going on here, Mr. Chernick," the nurse said cheerfully.

"How long will he be gone?" Dan asked.

"At least two hours."

"Can I wait here?"

"Sure. He might want the company when he gets back."

Dan realized he hadn't set up his flight yet, and he was determined to return to Jacksonville in time to see his new granddaughter. After making several calls and booking a 2:30 p.m. flight, Dan leaned his head back in the chair and slowly exhaled.

Soon he drifted into a deep sleep.

# CHAPTER SIXTEEN

## *Day of Reckoning*

"Mr. Lucas. Mr. Lucas."

Dan felt a gentle nudge on his shoulder as he struggled to wake from a sound sleep. The attractive face of a slender brunette with soft features and warm brown eyes greeted his tired eyes.

"Mr. Lucas, I'm Ruth Williams, Ben's daughter."

Dan was confused. "You're here! I thought you were going to call me when you were ready to leave Jacksonville. What time is it?"

"It's ten past one in the afternoon. I did call—you didn't answer your phone."

Dan pulled out his phone and saw that the battery was dead. "Oh, I'm sorry. I forgot to charge my phone with all of the excitement."

"That's all right. You must be exhausted."

"Yeah, I haven't slept much in the last couple days."

"Thank you so much for looking after Dad."

"Oh, it was my pleasure. I've never met anyone quite like him. We were having a pretty intense conversation last night before he got sick. By the way, where is he?"

"He's still at the cath lab. I guess they had problems with the procedure and are still working on him."

"I'm sorry to hear that."

"Oh, no. I'm relieved they have him stable and are going to find out where the blockage is. He's pretty tough and he's been through a lot more than this. He was a wrestling champion in high school and college."

"What? Are you kidding? He never mentioned that!"

"He keeps a lot to himself. If his heart and lungs hold out, he should make it. Maybe now I can convince him to quit smoking. Have you known my father long?"

"Actually, we met only yesterday. The storm kept us in the terminal all night and I had a chance to get to know a lot about him. He's a very determined man."

"Yes, he is—and full of surprises too. I'm very grateful to you for contacting me. My husband and I never thought this day would come."

"Your father obviously cares about you. I think he's trying to turn over a new leaf."

"We both are. Maybe now we can start fresh."

"I'm sure you will. When do you think they'll be done working on him?"

"The nurse said in about another hour or so. Please don't feel obligated to wait. I'm sure you have a flight to catch."

"Actually, I do. My youngest daughter is in labor with her first baby. I need to get home before the big event."

"I have your number, Mr. Lucas. I'll be in touch as soon as I have some news about Dad."

"Don't forget to pray for him," Dan said. "Your dad and I talked about a lot last night, and I hope I got through to him."

Ruth looked puzzled, but then smiled. "Don't worry. I'll work on him too. We have a lot of catching up to do, as you may have heard."

"I did, and I'm very glad I had a chance to meet you. Tell your father I want to hear from him soon."

"I will. God bless you, Mr. Lucas, and safe travels."

***

Dan felt a sense of relief as he left the hospital in a Yellow Cab and returned to the now bustling Charlotte terminal, his backpack in hand. Ben would be all right, and Dan might even make it home before Sienna gave birth. His fatigue was lifting, along with his spirits.

The cancelled and rescheduled flights created long waiting lines at every gate. With an hour to wait before the boarding of his flight, Dan stopped in a terminal restaurant to eat a good meal before the trip home. As he passed by the bar to take a table at the back of the eatery, a disheveled, hunched-over individual turned and looked directly at him.

*Good Lord, what's happened to him? Talk about being in hell!*

Stan Crofton, with bloodshot eyes and a drink in hand, motioned for Dan to have a seat next to him.

*Looks like he needs help, bad.* Reluctantly, Dan sat down.

Gone was the swagger and arrogance. A now defeated and deflated Stan Crofton gave a pleading look to Dan and fought back tears, while a server stepped up to Dan's table.

"What's happened, Stan? Is the family okay?" Dan asked after ordering a soda and a sandwich.

"They arrested Richie this morning—right in the hospital. He tried to kidnap his girlfriend—that idiot. He thought he could pump me for more money and make his troubles go away." Stan shook his head and stared down into his drink.

"What hospital? And what was he doing there? Is he okay?"

"Mercy Medical Center. His girlfriend's pregnant, but it sounds like she told him about it only yesterday. During his escapade, I guess the stress got to her and she might lose the baby. She started having pains and he drove her there to get help."

Dan shook his head. "I'm sorry, Stan."

Dan was shocked. Stan had always projected an image of wealth and success. He made sure everyone knew he had waterfront property in Annapolis, Maryland, and after retirement, he took a high-profile national security job where he took credit for the work of others from his previous NCIS career. Most of all, Stan had always presented his wife and kids as paragons of virtue. He often bragged to colleagues that he sent his kids to the finest schools—and now he was on the verge of a breakdown. Dan felt sorry for him.

"Do you want to talk about it?" Dan asked after a long silence.

Stan shrugged. "I wasn't here for a business meeting. I came here to try to get Richie into rehab. He got hooked on oxycodone after his motorcycle accident. Jean and I knew something was wrong when his grades started to fall, but then they shot back up. That devious kid learned how to hack into the school's computer and insert phony grades into the database. We sent him money for three semesters before we figured out he wasn't in school anymore. We were paying for his drug habit."

"Wow, I'm surprised to hear that. But he was doing the right thing, getting his girlfriend help. That isn't how selfish, mean addicts think, Stan. I'll bet he's a good young man at heart. And, he's in trouble over his head."

Stan's laugh was harsh. He gulped his drink and looked Dan in the eye. "You always had it together and I was just an act. I was jealous—that's why I made the call to the IG on you. I couldn't compete. All your stuff always worked, and I never got anything off the ground. I guess my kids got all my bad habits, too. I know it's too late, but I'm sorry." Crofton took a deep breath. "I'm getting what I deserve."

Dan almost couldn't believe his ears. But he didn't feel vindicated; he felt sad for Crofton and his son. He ordered another soda and studied Stan.

"Apology accepted. I knew it was you, but that's water under the bridge now. You know, the whole thing actually made me a better agent. After the 2B, I got a whole lot better administratively, and that helped me later on. Don't worry, Stan. Life's too short to carry around grudges, and it's about time I let go of it too. Don't give up on Richie. I bet he's going to be all right."

"He's gonna have plenty of time to think about it in jail. I'm not gonna bail him out this time. He's gonna have to sit in his cell and kick his habit the hard way. He's got to hit bottom and want to get clean before I can help him. It's about time he grew up. I need to let go so he can become a man."

"How about his girlfriend?"

"She's upset, but she won't press charges—she still loves him. She knew the drugs were controlling him. That's why she left him. She still cares about him. But he needs to get clean. Doctors aren't so sure about the baby, though. Her mother arrived at the hospital, so I left. Figured I'd be in the way."

"What can I do to help?" Dan asked.

"Nothing, Dan. Your friendship is more than enough. I know I don't deserve it, but I appreciate you burying the hatchet. I've cried on your shoulder enough now. I know you need to get home to your family. Stay in touch, and I'll do the same. I mean it."

"How about I keep you all in my prayers? You've got a long road, but it can be done. I've seen it done. Good luck, Stan."

After bidding Crofton farewell, Dan grabbed his phone to call Connie and realized he hadn't charged it. He strode back out into the concourse before collapsing in a heap next to a charging station. His mind was a blur, but his body felt light, as if a great weight had been lifted off his shoulders. He thought about Crofton for a long time and realized he'd finally let go of the hate. *I'm making progress.*

When he checked his watch, he realized he'd been sitting for almost a half hour in a state of mental shutdown. He quickly got up and hurried to the gate, arriving as the delayed flight started to board. For a second, Dan considered the consequences of missing the flight home, but he snapped his thoughts back to the present and called Connie to let her know he was on his way. He'd be in Jacksonville, God willing, before suppertime. Hopefully before baby time, too.

*I'm gonna make it.* With boarding pass in hand, he negotiated the crowded aisle of the fully booked flight. Most of the passengers looked haggard and exhausted. After reaching his seat, he hoisted his backpack into the overhead bin and felt the vibration of his phone on his hip.

"Mr. Lucas?"

Dan recognized Ruth Williams' voice, but it had a tight, distraught quality to it.

"Yes, Ruth. How's your dad?"

"He passed away five minutes ago; he went into cardiac arrest again and they couldn't resuscitate him. Thank you for calling me so I could be with my father during his last hours." Ruth quietly sobbed into the phone. "He was a good man."

Dan felt like he'd been hit with a two-by-four. "I'm so sorry. Thank you for letting me know."

"Good-bye, Dan Lucas."

# CHAPTER SEVENTEEN

## *Full Circle*

A warm Florida afternoon sunbathed the palm trees in Dan's front yard with a golden light.

He leaned down to open the mailbox with one hand while he balanced a bag of last-minute Christmas gifts in his other. The box was full. He struggled to pull out the bundle of Christmas cards and letters neatly bound with a rubber band. Christmas Eve had arrived and the mailman had just deposited the final haul of Christmas greetings for the year.

As Dan walked up the driveway of his Florida-style Jacksonville home, he surveyed the neatly trimmed lawn and shrubs in the landscaping and deemed the house presentable for the holidays. The house was his retirement castle, a not-so-modest rambler with two extra bedrooms where his daughters camped out on their frequent overnight visits.

He and Connie had put a lot of work into this year's Christmas decorations. Dan paused for a minute to admire the strings of lights adorning the two tall Italian cypress trees that flanked the porch and framed Connie's big wreath on the front door.

He quietly snuck into the foyer, making sure he wasn't seen. The loud, cheerful sounds of babies and women talking in the distance filled the house. Dan stealthily disappeared into the master bedroom to hide the goodies in his closet.

After safely secreting the bags, he strolled into the family room and put the mail on the kitchen counter, which was covered with plates of cookies and baby bottles. Two of his daughters noticed his arrival.

"Hi, Daddy!" they both said.

Dan eagerly joined his growing brood.

Connie and their three daughters were on the floor, playing with the babies. Sarah's son, Aaron, now sixteen months old, ran through the family room hoping to entice Grandpa into chasing him—a game he loved to play over and over again.

Samantha, their oldest daughter who was visiting from California, held her twenty-five-month-old son, Brandon, and Sienna watched Jessica, now eight months old, totter toward a toy that Aaron had dropped. Dan had made it back in time to be at the hospital before Jessica arrived.

"Man, this place looks like a bomb hit it," he joked as he picked his way through the toys strewn over the floor. He beheld his wife and daughters with pride as they tended to the young ones. Being a grandpa was just fine!

Dan had settled into a comfortable routine after getting home from his trip to Germany and his ordeal with Ben. Even after months had passed, Dan still felt a sense of loss and grief when he relived the events at the Charlotte airport. He often thought about Ben; some nights he would wake up in a cold sweat after dreaming about Ben in a dark, mournful place.

Those were the hours when Dan went into the den to work on his book, which would be released in the coming year.

Ben had been his sounding board, but also the catalyst for Dan's completing the book. So many people didn't know the Lord and so many didn't understand why it was so important. When the Christian publisher had accepted his manuscript, he was sure the Lord wanted things that way.

Dan sifted through the mail and put the many cards with familiar names into a pile. One caught his eye; it had no return address. He opened it. A color photo of Stan Crofton and his family had a greeting written on the front in thick black ink. A fit and healthy-looking Richie and his sister, Rebecca, were smiling in the photo taken in front of a docked sailboat.

"I'll be headed to Jacksonville in February. I'll look you up and we can talk. Merry Christmas. Stan, Jean, Richie, and Rebecca."

*Hmm. That's interesting*, Dan thought. *Looks like he was sincere. Glad he made the effort to stay in touch.*

After his contract job had ended, Dan busied himself with his reading, his regular gym workouts, his book, and his growing tasks as a grandfather. With two of his three daughters living within five miles of Connie and him, Dan nearly always had a grandchild at home to spoil.

No more contract work. Instead, Dan had widened his reading of Christian topics and gotten serious about his book. He also joined a Bible study class at his local church, and for the first time he started to discuss his views with his pastors and friends.

\*\*\*

Christmas arrived at the Lucas household with a suddenness that Dan was becoming accustomed to as he grew older. The days blended into weeks, and the weeks turned into months more rapidly every year. Increasingly mindful of his own mortality, Dan strove to make the most of every day, and that usually meant time with his family and Bible research.

This Christmas was special—all of his daughters, grandchildren, and sons-in-law were together for the first time. Connie and the girls cooked a fabulous turkey dinner with all the trimmings, and after gorging themselves on the sumptuous meal, the men settled into the family room to watch football.

As Dan positioned himself in his favorite recliner—affectionately referred to by all as "the throne"—he heard his cell phone ring in the nearby study. On any other day, Dan would have let the call go to voicemail; however, he felt an unexplained urge to answer it.

Dan picked up his phone and noticed the incoming number wasn't one he recognized.

The voice said, "Merry Christmas."

"Merry Christmas. Who is this?" Dan asked. The caller had a familiar voice, but he couldn't place it.

"It's Ben. Ben Chernick."

Dan nearly dropped the phone. "Who is this? This isn't funny!" He could feel his fury building. *What a cruel, cruel joke.*

"Dan, it's me, I assure you. I know you're surprised to hear from me. I should have called sooner."

"Surprised! But your daughter … she said you passed away after I left the hospital." In a harsh tone, Dan said, "Who is this?"

"Remember our talks in the airport? You so clearly laid out your case for God and the afterlife. I gave you a hard time, but I listened, and you talked—for hours."

"How can this be? Ruth clearly told me you were dead when she called, and then I didn't hear from anyone again. I assumed your daughter was grieving, so I never bothered her. How can you be alive?"

"The doctors tell me it was a medical miracle. I came back about fourteen minutes after they had given up attempts to resuscitate me. They had already declared me dead and covered me with a sheet. Ruth was still in the room when an orderly came in to take me to the morgue. They say my heart started again on its own. I have no aftereffects, no brain damage—I'm fine. The doctors can't believe it."

Dan's mind raced to recall the past. He remembered saying a silent prayer for Ben after being seated on the plane. Afterward he had an odd sense of calm, but he chalked it up to being a side effect of sheer exhaustion and mild shock.

"Why didn't you call me? You waited eight months to tell me you survived?"

"In all the excitement, Ruth lost her cell phone at the airport on the way back—she never found it, so she didn't have your number. Since you have an unlisted number and don't have any info on the Net, it took me a while to find you. Plus, I needed some time to think and to rebuild my relationship with Ruth and Tim, and they had the additional grief of losing Tim's brother, Rob, on the same day we were stranded together."

"Oh, I'm sorry to hear that." Dan's mind was still racing, but he was beginning to control his emotions better and focus on Ben's words.

"As painful as his death has been to Tim and Ruth, Rob is partly the reason all this happened to me."

"How's that?"

"Remember all those power failures we had at the airport that we thought were caused by the storm?"

"Yeah?"

"I found out they were triggered when Tim's brother, Rob, crashed his truck into an electrical substation near the airport. If the power hadn't kept going off and triggering my episodes, I might not have had the heart attack and ended up staying down here. You're right—I don't believe in coincidences anymore."

Dan's mind continued to swirl with a mixture of shock and elation. He strained to retain his focus and carry on a coherent conversation. "Are you calling from Philly?"

"No, Palm Coast."

Ben's tone of voice was much lighter and warmer than Dan remembered. "Palm Coast? Are you visiting your daughter for Christmas?"

"Actually, I never left. Ruth brought me here from Charlotte to recuperate. I'm living here for the time being and getting to know my grandson and son-in-law. I feel like I finally have a real family now. Tim finished seminary and has his own church. It's small but growing, and I've got a part-time job—an outreach project to the Jewish community."

"Wow! I thought once a Jew, always a Jew."

"Oh, I'm still Jewish. But like you so eloquently pointed out, Jesus was a Jew and a rabbi, so I'm not jumping ship. We're on the same team—it's just that he's the coach, and I'm coming off the bench ...." Ben took a breath. "We need to talk."

"That's great," Dan said, "but what about your classes?"

"I took an extended sabbatical—long overdue. The campus was partially destroyed by the tornado and school didn't reopen for months. Besides, I'm getting my priorities straight. Are you busy next week?"

"No ...." Dan's mind was still reeling. *Ben's alive!*

"How about coming down here for a day or two? It'll be worth your time."

"I'd be glad to. I'd like to see Ruth again and meet her husband. We need to—"

Dan stopped in mid-sentence and his mind raced to piece together the events that had led to Ben's collapse, death, and miraculous recovery.

"Dan? Dan?"

Ben was greeted by silence.

"Look," Ben said, "I know I should have tried to reach you before, but I've needed time to think and digest what happened to me. By the way, I'm celebrating my first Christmas today. You know, it took our chat and my mortality to wake me up, but to be honest, my heart attack changed me in more ways than just living a healthy lifestyle. Your view of life and eternity is more accurate than you could ever imagine."

Instantly, Dan's mind cleared. "You had an NDE! You had an NDE!" he shouted.

"Like I said, Dan. Get down here. We've a lot to talk about."

Dan could hear Ben's smile.

Jeff Walton

Final Departure

# About the Author

Jeff Walton, a graduate of West Chester University, is a US Navy Vietnam veteran and retired US Naval Criminal Investigative Service (NCIS) special agent who spent more than thirty-four years in federal law enforcement and national security work.

His career assignments ranged from felony criminal investigations to counterintelligence and combating terrorism operations and investigations in the United States, the Far East, and Europe.

He also served in senior management positions at NCIS Headquarters, the Office of the Assistant Secretary of Defense for C3I, the National Counterintelligence Center, and the Office of the National Counterintelligence Executive.

He and his wife live in Florida.

Final Departure

Dear Reader,

Thank you for reading my book.

I hope you found *Final Departure* to be both entertaining and stimulating. I learned a great deal during the research phase of the book. I am neither a Bible scholar nor a clergyman; I'm simply a student of the Bible.

I have assembled information that I believe will help you to better grasp some of the key areas of research and commentary that a relatively small group of Christian scholars continue to focus on in search of the truth.

I am planning a new book in the Dan Lucas series, so please keep an eye online for my next work. My website is www.jeffwaltonbooks.com.

If you enjoyed the book, please do me the great favor of writing a review. You can do so at www.Amazon.com.

If you have a question or comment, you can contact me at jeffwaltonbooks@gmail.com.

Sincerely,

Jeff Walton

Final Departure

# Ordering Information

### Final Departure
by Jeff Walton

ISBN: 978-0-9974334-0-1

Sunbrook Publishing
PO Box 730
St. Augustine, FL  32085
www.JeffWaltonBooks.com
JeffWaltonBooks@gmail.com

Printed in the USA
CPSIA information can be obtained
at www.ICGtesting.com
LVHW090408090224
771185LV00049B/923